"I don't like this," said Lane. "The damned animal ought to be doing something."

The creature came to a complete stop, and Lane found himself within a thousand miles before he could bring the Deathmaker to a halt.

"Damn it!" he muttered. "Why doesn't it move?"

With an enormous effort of will he forced his hand back to the acceleration controls and began approaching the creature.

The creature began retreating, and finally burst from the cloud into open space.

"What's he doing out there, Lane?" asked the Mariner.

They both looked at the creature in the viewscreen—and as they did so, it stopped drifting away and began approaching them.

"Let's run," said the Mariner.

Lane wanted to; he wasn't used to fear, but decided the only way to conquer it was to meet it head-on.

He moved his hand—and fired a blast into the creature . . .

All the fear and apprehension he had felt vanished, to be replaced with something strange and alien and painful that threatened to tear his consciousness to pieces.

☆   ☆   ☆

"Resnick has a beautiful style."
—*Science Fiction & Fantasy Book Review*

Turn the page for more raves for Mike Resnick . . .

☆

"Resnick is exceptional . . . fun, too."
—*Baltimore Sun*

☆

"He's addictive. . . . Mike Resnick is one of the
best storytellers to hit science fiction in years."
—**Frank M. Robinson**

☆

"Mike Resnick has written excellent
space adventures."
—*Locus*

☆

"Resnick is a reader's writer, one who can be
counted upon to deliver a dependably
entertaining read."
—**Michael Kube-McDowell**

☆

"Mike Resnick spins a great yarn."
—**Jerry Pournelle**

☆

"You may come away from Mike Resnick's
books with considerably more than
a rousing good tale."
—**Jo Clayton**

MIKE RESNICK

THE SOUL EATER

WARNER BOOKS

A Time Warner Company

WARNER BOOKS EDITION

Questar is a registered trademark of Warner Books, Inc.

This Warner Books Edition is published by arrangement with the author.

Cover illustration by Dorian Vallejo
Cover design by Don Puckey

Warner Books, Inc.
1271 Avenue of the Americas
New York, NY 10020

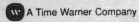 A Time Warner Company

Printed in the United States of America

First Warner Books Printing: July, 1992

10 9 8 7 6 5 4 3 2 1

To Carol, as always,

And to my daughter, Laura,
With love and aggravation

PROLOGUE

There is a world, toward the core of the galaxy, where the evening sky is so bright that most of the cities—outposts, really—have never bothered to install artificial illumination. The stellar configurations are all different, and sophisticated astronomy is extremely difficult, but if you look very carefully through a powerful telescope you can just barely see our sun, the tiny wart at the tip of a constellation known as the Witch's Nose.

The name of the world is Northpoint, though it is neither north nor pointed. It consists of a lot of land, a little water, a pair of mountain ranges, one huge canyon, and seven Tradertowns, small outposts consisting of bars, restaurants, survey offices, banks, hotels, brothels, dope dens, and radio centers. The permanent populations of the Tradertowns consist of the employees and (infrequently) the owners of these establishments; the transient populations, which are occasionally non-existent and sometimes enormous but usually somewhere in between, consist of traders, miners, explorers, prospectors, gamblers, cargo loaders, a few of the bolder and hardier scientists, and a handful of other wanderers, wayfarers, adventurers, and misfits. They hail from all across the galaxy, though their seed traces back to Earth, and they have very little in common other than a love of desolation and a continually receding vision of instant riches.

On Northpoint, the smallest, grubbiest, grimiest of the Tradertowns is Hellhaven, which makes sporadic efforts to live up to its name; and in Hellhaven, the only building capable of holding more than thirty people at once is Tchaka's Emporium.

Tchaka's is primarily a tavern, specializing in the most exotic concoctions of a thousand worlds, but depending on which level and room you are at in the unbelievable maze of levels and rooms it is also an opium den, a whorehouse, a currency exchange, and an antiquarian cartographic chart shop.

But it is the bar at Tchaka's that is the social and financial center of Hellhaven. Here men and women of every background and color—including some that have never been seen on Earth—meet and bargain and occasionally battle; here traders speaking more than ten thousand tongues wheel and deal, more by signs and signals and grimaces than by words; here used-up old men live out their final pitifully short years, swapping lies about the Dreamwish Beast and other monsters of the rapidly growing mythology of the spaceways; here, in this strange-smelling, ill-lit marketplace, one can buy anything that possesses a cash value, from gold to flesh to virtue.

And it is here, in Tchaka's bar, that we shall begin our story, since it is here, more than four millennia after Man first left his home system, that Nicobar Lane began his strange, haunted pursuit of the Soul Eater.

CHAPTER

I

Tchaka's was crowded.

At the bar sat a trio of prospectors from Rakhvad, their bluish skins glistening like no other human subspecies; a pair of traders, brilliantly dressed with the spoils of their latest dealings, huddled over a small table near the door, where the lighting would make them brighter still; in the back of the tavern, playing *jabob*—an offshoot of blackjack, with a 52-48 break for the house—were five members of the native humanoid race of Dabih Minor, with their wide-set cat's eyes and almost nonexistent ears. Two of the whores from another part of the building were taking a beer break, casting don't-you-dare-come-hither glares at anyone who chanced to look in their direction. Men with money and men without, scaly men and hairy men, the momentarily rich and the momentarily poor, all squeezed and jammed themselves into Tchaka's.

Into this mass of humanity and semihumanity stepped Ector Allsworth, a portly, balding man of enormous proportions and a deathly gray cast to his leathery skin. He looked prosperous, even by the boom-or-bust standards of the Tradertowns. His yellow eyes scanned the room for a moment, and then he walked over to the bar. The bartender pointed to a lone man sitting at a small table in the farthest and darkest of the oddly shaped tavern's many corners. Allsworth nodded his thanks and walked over to the man.

"Is this yours?" he asked, dropping a small, pale-gold business card onto the table.

The man stared at it for a moment.

NICOBAR LANE
—I KILL THINGS—
HELLHAVEN, NORTHPOINT

"What can I do for you?" said Lane, slowly sipping his Cygnian cognac.

"Mr. Lane," said Allsworth, "I won't mince words. My name is Ector Allsworth, and I represent the Vainmill Syndicate."

"Never heard of it."

"I don't doubt it. They're one of a number of holding companies controlled by Ilse Vescott. Does that name mean anything to you?"

"You're looking at me as if it should," said Lane.

"She's just about the richest woman in the entire Deluros system," said Allsworth.

"That's a long way from here," said Lane. "This is the frontier, Mr. Allsworth. You'll have to forgive us if we don't keep up to date on the social and financial doings back at Deluros. However, I am properly impressed with your credentials, so please go on with whatever proposition you have in mind."

"Among the more philanthropic aspects of the Vainmill Syndicate are a number of museums and zoos," said Allsworth. "I have been told that you're the best hunter in this area, and there are a number of specimens we need at this time.''

''You must understand, Mr. Allsworth,'' said Lane, ''that I never supply specimens to zoos. 'Hunter' is perhaps too broad a term.''

''If you're not a hunter, just what are you?''

''A killer,'' said Lane, taking another sip of his drink. ''That's what I do for a living: I kill things. Which does not preclude my working for your museums. What is it that you need so desperately that you came all the way to Northpoint?''

''First off, I need three dozen Sillyworms,'' said Allsworth.

''Not impossible,'' said Lane. ''How much are you prepared to pay?''

''Five thousand credits apiece.''

''Unacceptable,'' said Lane. ''The people out here don't have too much faith in the longevity of your Democracy. Credits aren't worth the paper they're printed on.''

''All right,'' said Allsworth. ''You name the currency.''

''The new-series Maria Theresa dollars they're using in the Corvus system.''

''The Corvus system!'' Allsworth exploded. ''That bunch of wild-eyed insurrectionists!''

''I don't give a damn about their politics,'' said Lane. ''Just their money. Twelve thousand dollars apiece.''

Allsworth seemed lost in thought for a moment, then looked up and nodded his head. ''I also need five Baffledivers.''

''You may have to wait a year or so for them.''

''Twenty thousand apiece, and a forty percent bonus if you can deliver them in four months.''

''The price is fair enough,'' said Lane. ''Forget about your bonus. It'll take more than a year. Anything else?''

''Just one thing,'' said Allsworth.

"I was wondering when you'd get around to it," said Lane, the trace of a smile on his lips.

"I don't quite know what you mean," said Allsworth.

"Sillyworms and Bafflledivers aren't exactly pedestrian, but they're not rare enough to cause a man of your obvious station in life to chase all the way to hell and gone just to tell me that you want them. We could have consummated this whole thing by radio. So you rather obviously want something else."

"You seem to think you know what it is," said Allsworth.

"Of course I know what it is," said Lane, irritated. "It's the only reason anyone ever comes out here to see me. You want me to hunt down the Dreamwish Beast."

Allsworth nodded. "We'll pay anything within reason."

"There's nothing reasonable about it. First of all, the odds are about twenty to one that the Dreamwish Beast is just a myth, a fable made up by some demented old cargo hand who cracked from the boredom and started believing in his nightmares. Second, if it really exists, it's the only life form we've ever run across that lives in space and the only one that eats energy. And if you know a way to kill something that eats energy, I'd be mighty indebted to you if you'd tell me about it."

"All I'm prepared to tell you about is how much we are willing to pay."

"Not interested. It's just a story to scare children with. Even the name is crazy. Look, we happen to live in a sexual universe. If there is one Dreamwish Beast, there's got to be more: a parent, an offspring, an original body that this creature split off from. But there isn't anything like that. There's just one Dreamwish Beast—which is paradoxical, which means there isn't any such thing."

"It's been spotted," said Allsworth.

"Bunk."

"I can give you its coordinates as of five days ago," said Allsworth.

"No you can't," said Lane. "What you *can* give me are the coordinates of some loony spacehand who fantasizes a little better than his shipmates."

"How does ten million credits or its equivalent in any currency you name sound to you?"

"Like a lot of money," said Lane. "Why don't you offer it to someone who feels like spending the rest of his life chasing a dream?"

"That's your answer?" said Allsworth.

"Of course that's my answer," said Lane.

"What if we pay your expenses while you hunt for it, once you've rounded up the other stuff?"

"Forget it," said Lane, rising. "I'll radio you once I've got your Sillyworms and let you know where I've dropped them off. I assume a message to the Vainmill Syndicate will reach you?"

"You won't reconsider?" asked Allsworth, also rising.

Lane shook his head. "Try asking some hunter who's out to make a name for himself and isn't too bright."

"We've got about two hundred of them," said Allsworth, trying to suppress a guilty smile.

"Why not?" Lane shrugged. "You're only going to have to pay one of them at the most." He shook Allsworth's hand and walked out onto the dusty unpaved street. The wind was blowing from the west, and as he walked the five hundred yards to his combination office and hangar, he had to pull down his facemask to protect his eyes from the flying dirt and sand.

Once there, he opened the door and walked directly to the antique desk which was tucked neatly into a corner of the room. It was covered by piles of papers: orders, some new, others dating back five and six years, all waiting to be filled.

He added Allsworth's requests to the pile, then lit a pipe and settled back in an easy chair, surrounded by tokens and mementoes of a quarter-century of stalking exotic creatures on even more exotic worlds.

He dozed for a few minutes, then awoke suddenly as he began choking on the smoke from the tobacco. He put the pipe out, rinsed his face off, opened a bottle of Alphard brandy, poured himself a small glass, and sat down at the desk, pen in hand. The *Deathmaker* was stripped down completely, its hull repaired and strengthened, its engines overhauled, its nuclear pile replaced, and he would have to equip it from scratch before going out again. He glanced over some of the orders and began estimating what he'd need: a laser cannon, two vibrators, a molecular imploder (if he could get his hands on one somewhere on Northpoint). There'd be the standard hand weapons: the stungun, the screecher, and an old-fashioned laser pistol. He checked his source books for the correct taxidermy kits for the various animals he planned to slay, computed the amount of food and air he'd need and then tripled it, marked down the proper star charts to incorporate into the ship's three-dimensional Carto-System.

Then he checked out the worlds he'd be visiting on this particular hunt—three oxygen, two chlorine, one methane, two ammonia, one unknown—and estimated the number and strength of the protective suits and systems he'd need. He also made a note to check the decontamination chamber and one of the airlocks that hadn't been functioning properly toward the end of the last hunt. Going over his back orders more thoroughly, he decided that he'd have enough cargo space for a five-month hunt, possibly six if he had trouble with the Devilowls.

Then came the crew. The Dabihs made the best skinners, and he decided to take a pair of them along. He considered hiring a chlorine-breather, but decided he'd waste too much time going to Asterion VIII—the nearest outpost of sentient chlorine-breathers—to make it worthwhile. As usual, he rejected the idea of adding a methane-breather to the crew; not only were they rare as hen's teeth, but they tended to shatter like so much glass if they weren't totally insulated from noise.

That left the Lord High Mufti, which was more mascot than crew member, more court jester than sailor, quite possibly insane if it had a mind at all, and a genuine hazard during all phases of a hunt. Still, he would have felt somehow incomplete without the Mufti, so he computed its food supply—live insects and dead reptiles—and jotted down a reminder to tranquilize it just before takeoff.

He made arrangements to leave in five days, which would give him time to hire his crew, equip his ship, and have one last fling at all the pleasures of Tchaka's, alcoholic and otherwise. . . .

CHAPTER

2

The Sillyworms giggled and howled and hooted all the way to Kakkab Kastu IV, the gigantic shipping center that handled most of the commerce in this section of the galaxy. The worms, averaging some twelve feet in length and possessing a paralyzing venom—in fact, Lane still couldn't understand why they weren't classified as poisonous snakes—never seemed to know when they were dead. If you shot them with a laser, or hit them with a toxic gas, they behaved like any other defunct animals; but if you killed one with an ultrasonic weapon it set up some sympathetic vibration deep within the animal, causing the corpse to giggle maniacally for months, and frequently years, after the Sillyworm was officially dead. Hence its name, and hence Lane's relief at getting them off the *Deathmaker*. He instructed the port authorities to ship his various kills off to their sundry purchasers, left the Mufti happily chattering to itself on the ceiling of his hotel room, and went out to dinner.

He remained in port for four days, until all his money for the most recent hunt had been cabled to him, then made preparations to pick up the Baffledivers in the Pinnipes system. He kept his crew intact and added a Gillsniffer to his staff; Baffledivers spent a lot of time under what passed for water on Pinnipes II, and he would probably need help in tracking them down. Gillsniffers didn't come cheaply—just finding an animal that could both survive space flight and follow an odor beneath a dozen fathoms of water and other liquids was hard enough, let alone training and domesticating it—but he knew where to look and what to spend, and it wasn't too long before he picked up a prime one.

Then it was off on the long, seemingly endless voyage to Pinnipes. He toyed with taking a Deepsleep for forty or fifty days but decided against leaving the Dabihs and the Mufti unsupervised. Both had cast covetous and hungry eyes at the Gillsniffer from time to time, and he'd spent too much money on the damned thing to risk losing it before the hunt was over. So he stayed awake, and ate, and slept, and read, and listened, and ran in place, and participated in a thousand other little rituals he had created over the quarter-century of his hurry-up-and-wait existence. When the boredom became too great he donned his space suit and walked around the *Deathmaker*'s hull or let the ship tow him through the void.

In fact, he was standing on the outside of the hull on the day he noticed the warning buoy, a huge red flare some half-billion miles out from Pinnipes. He immediately reentered the ship and walked to the radio panel. When he was unable to find any Mayday broadcast on any of the frequencies he switched on his transmitting device.

"This is the *Deathmaker*, fifty-three Galactic Standard days out of Kakkab Kastu IV, headed for Pinnipes II, Nicobar Lane commanding. What seems to be the problem?"

There was a pause of perhaps five minutes, followed by a reply bristling with static:

"We read you, *Deathmaker*. The Pinnipes system is off limits since the discovery of a black hole in the position of a binary. All traffic to Pinnipes is being urged to return to its home base."

"Oh, shit," muttered Lane. "Not another one." He logged

the black hole on his Carto-System, then had the computer log a course to Pinnipes II that would avoid its fierce attraction. The computer came up with three courses; one was too dangerous, but the other two seemed to bypass the black hole very comfortably.

"This is *Deathmaker*," he said into the microphone. "I am proceeding to Pinnipes II, in search of Baffledivers, which I am duly licensed to hunt. I expect to be there for the better part of two Standard months, after which time I will radio you again."

He broke contact and fed the course he had chosen into the navigational computer. He was getting sick and tired of black holes cropping up more and more frequently. Once they were merely a theory, then a rare phenomenon; but it was now estimated that there were well over 100,000 black holes in the galaxy, and literally billions upon billions of them in the universe. They were collapsed stars, huge giants that had created such immense gravitational fields that they did not stop even at the neutron star stage, but continued collapsing upon themselves until all the laws of the normal universe were broken. No light could escape from a black hole, and it could gobble up planets millions of times its own size. It was theorized that if a man could survive inside the event horizon—that section beyond which light could not escape—time and space would become totally meaningless. Some theorists opted for the existence of white holes as well—holes somehow connected to the black holes, in which all the stellar material and garbage they devoured reappeared elsewhere and formed new stars—but thus far none had been observed, and the theory was fast falling into disrepute.

The philosophy and theories of black holes, however, did not interest Lane in the least. His sole concern was avoiding them, and, more particularly, the thirty-eight-mile hole currently on the far side of Pinnipes.

His approach took him the better part of a day. As he

entered an elliptical orbit around Pinnipes II, he began checking out the islands dotting the filthy liquid where he would be doing his hunting, searching for the one that would afford him the best shelter, the safest landing field, and the least chance of being caught up in one of the tidal waves that regularly raced across the planet, sometimes reaching heights of more than a mile.

He was just about to begin his descent when his ship told him that he was no longer alone.

Someone was about 150,000 miles off and above his port bow, inside the orbit of Pinnipes II. It didn't read like a ship, but there were a lot of races in the galaxy, and not all of them used the type of material that his sensing devices were programmed to read.

He switched on his radio.

"This is the *Deathmaker*, place of origin Northpoint, race of Man. Who are you?"

He repeated the signal at regular intervals but received no acknowledgment. He hadn't really expected any, but he was disappointed anyway, for it meant that he would have to delay his hunt for awhile. He hadn't survived this long by being incautious, and he had no intention of immobilizing himself on the planet until he had determined the identity and intentions of what he now assumed to be an alien ship.

He broke out of his orbit and began slowly approaching the ship. It withdrew from him at a leisurely pace. He increased his speed and flicked off the various safety switches on his laser cannon.

The alien ship continued retreating in the direction of the star, and now Lane began to worry in earnest. If it didn't alter its course in the next couple of hours it would be too close to the star for him to follow. That would lead to two inescapable conclusions: that the alien ship was impervious to the heat and radiation of a star, and that it would realize the limitations of the *Deathmaker*.

He followed it for another hour, and when it showed no sign of veering off on a tangent to Pinnipes, he took the initiative by increasing his speed and changing his course to take a position above the plane of the ecliptic. He didn't know whether the alien ship would pass above, beneath, or beside the star, but at least he'd be able to track it from his new vantage point.

He also attempted a spectroscopic analysis of the ship but drew an absolute blank. It was puzzling. His sensing devices told him that he was chasing a very real object, but neither they nor any other instrument aboard the *Deathmaker* could give him the slightest information about its makeup.

"*Deathmaker*, we have been reading your signals," said a static-ridden voice. "Who are you trying to raise? We cannot detect any other ships in your locale."

"There's something out there," said Lane. "I have just begun chasing it. Now will you kindly shut the hell up so this guy doesn't feel surrounded and maybe begin using his weapons?"

He flicked off his radio once more and turned back to his sensing panel, trying those basic tests he was acquainted with to determine exactly what he was chasing. He came up with a series of blanks.

When he reached his vantage point above and well beyond Pinnipes, he had the computer plot the alien ship's course. It was going to pass under the star, and he quickly laid in an intercept course. He spent the next few minutes tending to the needs of his inhuman passengers. Then, when the *Death-maker* had stabilized at its preselected intercept point, he sat back, his hand on the mechanism that would fire the laser cannon, and waited for the alien ship to appear.

It took him almost half an hour to realize that the ship had anticipated him and, once hidden from his sensors by Pinnipes, had immediately changed course and was heading in the general direction of the black hole at an increased speed. He immediately laid in a compensating course, designed to take him as close as possible to the hole.

When he arrived he couldn't see the hole at all, which wasn't too surprising. His instruments found it, though—a super gravitational field surrounded by small amounts of gas and debris which had taken up orbit around it.

"We still pick up no reading, *Deathmaker*," said the voice on his radio. "Are you sure you're not tracking some sort of reflection?"

"When's the last time you heard of something making that kind of reflection in space?" asked Lane disgustedly. "Besides, it's heading right into the black hole. Let me give you its coordinates and then maybe you'll get off my back."

"We have its coordinates," said the voice some five minutes later, "and have projected its course, on the unlikely assumption that it really exists. However, our instruments still can't find anything out there."

"Then you'd better get some new instruments," said Lane, "because it's within a million miles of the hole right now."

The alien ship seemed totally unaware that it was on a collision course—or absorption course, amended Lane—with the black hole. Not that it mattered any longer. From this distance, not even Pinnipes itself would be able to escape its grasp.

And then something strange happened. The alien ship's velocity should have been increasing as it was sucked nearer and nearer to the event horizon, but instead its speed remained unchanged. Then, when it was perhaps five hundred miles away from the black hole, it veered off and avoided the hole altogether.

"You guys must be wrong," said Lane, switching on his radio again. "That thing can't be a black hole."

"Why not?" said the voice a few minutes later.

"Because the ship just escaped from its field." He explained in detail what had happened.

"There is definitely a black hole there," said the voice. "It has been charted, logged, and scientifically examined. Since our instruments did not register your supposed alien vessel, we are forced to conclude that your ship's sensing devices are in error."

Lane broke off communications, walked down to his cargo hold, selected a small probe, and attached a long-duration space flare to it. Then he released it in the direction of the black hole. His instruments followed its flight as it approached the hole, while he himself was able to watch the glare of the flare through his viewing screen. It vanished from sight the instant it passed the event horizon, and his tracking panel lost all trace of it at the same moment.

Which meant that there *was* a black hole after all.

Which also meant that the alien ship had broken every physical law he knew of.

He opened his radio again. "Is there anything that would be immune to the gravitational field of a black hole?"

"No," came the reply. "Even light can't escape from it."

"That's not what I mean," said Lane. "Is there anything that would be immune to the gravitational *pull* of a black hole prior to entering it?"

"Nothing solid," was his answer. "Maybe x-rays or some forms of energy, though I doubt it. Nothing else."

"Which of these things wouldn't show up on your instrument board?" asked Lane.

"We'd pick up x-rays, that's for sure. At this distance we might miss some of the more exotic forms of energy, especially if they were partially or completely into the infra-red portion of the spectrum."

"Has any ship you've ever heard of been constituted of energy?" asked Lane.

"Nope. I'd check your ship's main computer banks for a malfunction if I were you."

"Everything's functioning perfectly," said Lane. "I just fired a probe into the hole and followed it every centimeter of the way."

"Well, *Deathmaker*, we have no other suggestions."

"I have," said Lane. "I think I just bumped into the Dreamwish Beast."

"Oh, hell," said the voice disgustedly. "Another crackpot. Now listen here, *Deathmaker*—don't you go spreading any crazy rumors about seeing the damned thing here. If there's one thing we don't need, it's ten thousand idiot trophy hunters falling into that black hole."

"No problem," said Lane. "I've got no interest in the Dreamwish Beast, if that's what it was. I'm here to hunt Baffledivers, and now that that thing—whatever it was—is gone, that's just what I'm going to do."

And, within another fifteen hours, he was walking across the floor of the murky ocean of Pinnipes II, his Gillsniffer's sonar signal pack in one hand and a stungun in the other, the day's adventure in space filed in that corner of his mind which was reserved for unimportant trivia to be withdrawn only when swapping tall tales at Tchaka's.

CHAPTER
3

It took Lane almost three months to round up his quota. Halfway through the hunt his Gillsniffer was attacked and killed by some denizen of the ocean, and he had to capture the rest of his prey unaided. But catch them he did, and another hunt was over. He dropped the Baffledivers off on a nearby shipping world and then, physically and mentally exhausted, he returned to Hellhaven.

He left the *Deathmaker* in its hangar, paid off the Dabihs, took a long nap, and, with the Mufti perched happily on his shoulder, he trudged down the dirt street to Tchaka's.

Tchaka himself was behind the bar, an impressive sight as always. He stood almost eight feet tall, his teeth were made of the finest and brightest gold, he wore a living lizard in his grotesquely stretched right earlobe, his bejeweled fingers glittered like ten tiny but brilliant suns, and he wore an intricately designed robe of some semimetallic fabric that seemed to change from primary to pastel and back again with his every movement. Perhaps most bizarre of all was his left eye: it was artificial, and it twinkled and sparkled with an equally artificial luminescence. It was originally rumored that the eye had been cut out in a knife fight during Hellhaven's infancy. Then it was whispered that it had been lost to some strange—

and possibly contagious—disease that was eating away at every inch of Tchaka's enormous body. The current theory was that Tchaka had gouged it out himself so that he could replace it with the wondrous orb that now resided inside his head, a notion Lane considered more terrifying than the other two stories, and more likely as well.

"Nicobar!" shouted Tchaka, looking up from his bartending duties. "Back from the wars and ready to spend your booty here?"

Lane smiled and walked over to the bar.

"You've been gone a long time, Nicobar," said Tchaka.

Lane nodded. "More than a year."

"Make a nice haul?"

"Pretty good. Fix me up something special."

"The first one's on the house," said Tchaka, shaking and mixing ingredients with the finesse of a concert pianist. "Is this all I can do for you? A year's a long time to be away from a lot of things, Nicobar," he added with a wink.

"I don't understand it," said Lane, shaking his head.

"What?"

"Why you wink with your good eye," said Lane. "Now, if it was me, I'd wink with the blind one."

"They're both good eyes, Nicobar," said Tchaka with a broad smile. "Don't you think they're pretty?"

"Gorgeous," said Lane, sampling the drink that Tchaka set before him. "But you can't see out of one of them."

"You think not?" said Tchaka. He closed his right eye and turned his flashing, blinking artificial eye toward the door. "A pair of men just walked in. The one on the left is about forty years old, bearded, wearing an old military uniform. The one on the right is a few years older, a little shorter, fat as all getout, clean-shaven, and, though you probably can't tell, he's missing most of his right leg."

"Well, I'll be damned!" said Lane, genuinely surprised. "What colors are they wearing?"

"I have absolutely no idea," said Tchaka, opening his right eye again. "So you're surprised, Nicobar!" He threw back his massive head and laughed. "That's more emotion than I've ever seen you show."

"How do you do it?" asked Lane.

"You thought this eye was just for beauty?" said Tchaka. "Nicobar, I'm surprised at you. What need does the proprietor of the best whorehouse on Northpoint have for beauty? No, my friend, this eyeball is more than a work of art: it's a work of science. It possesses both infrared and ultraviolet lenses and is tied in to my optic nerve endings. Poor Nicobar, with only the two eyes God gave him! Poor, poor man, who only sees the surface of things, while Tchaka sees colors and shapes that you can't even imagine!"

"I'm impressed," said Lane.

"Come, Nicobar," said Tchaka, leaning over the bar. "Look deeply into it, and see the secrets of all time and space."

Lane was about to peer closely into the shining orb when the Mufti tensed, digging its claws into his shoulder. He straightened up immediately.

"Some other time, Tchaka."

"What's the mater?"

"My pet just saw the lizard in your ear. If you get any closer you're going to have the opportunity to let science do for your hearing what it did for your vision."

"An ultrasonic ear to go along with my eye," said Tchaka, toying with the idea. "I'll sleep on that one, Nicobar. And now, can I arrange something for *you* to sleep on, my friend?"

"Later," said Lane, sipping at his drink.

"Whatever you wish," said Tchaka. "Anything for my old friend Nicobar."

"Until he runs out of money," said Lane dryly.

"You must never confuse friendship with loyalty," said

Tchaka. "I am friendly to everyone, but I am loyal only to Tchaka's interests."

"Reasonable," said Lane.

"I am all things to all men," said Tchaka easily. "To you I am reasonable. To someone else I am unfathomable and unknowable. Would you believe," he continued, grinning and grinding his fingers into the hardwood bar, leaving fingerprint indentations almost a centimeter deep in it, "that to some people I am actually a figure of terror?"

"I can't imagine why," said Lane, wondering if any other man in the galaxy could match strength with Tchaka.

"And to some," continued Tchaka, "I am a man of total mystery."

"I never thought of you as being especially mysterious," said Lane. "But speaking of mysteries, I've got a little one to share with you. What do you know about black holes?"

"Black, white, pink, red, brown, polka-dot, they're all the same to Tchaka," he replied with a lecherous grin that showed off his golden teeth to best advantage.

"Seriously," said Lane, "do you know anything about them?"

"Tchaka knows a little something about almost everything."

"Including black holes?"

"Including black holes."

"What would you say if I told you that something I was chasing got within five hundred miles of one and then veered away?"

"I'd say you were wrong," said Tchaka, without hesitation.

"I wasn't wrong," said Lane.

"What did it look like?" asked Tchaka.

"I don't know. I was too far away to see it."

"Then how do you know it was there, Nicobar?"

"My ship's sensors followed it all the way to the hole," said Lane.

"What happened to it after it avoided the hole?"

Lane shrugged. "I don't know. It left the system and I went back to work."

"You weren't curious?"

"Not enough to go after it," said Lane. "Besides, if it could buck a black hole's gravitational field, my ship wasn't likely to be much of a match for it."

"Probably not," agreed Tchaka, sucking thoughtfully on a bottle.

"Ever hear of anything like that?" asked Lane.

"Just once," said Tchaka.

"Oh? From who?"

"Old man in the corner," said Tchaka, nodding toward an ancient, wrinkled man who sat motionless at a table, a huge bottle of almost pure alcohol beside his elbow. "It was thirty years ago, maybe even forty. He came in one day and got rip-roaring drunk. It wasn't so busy in those days, so I helped him sober up. He talked all night and most of the morning about something that ducked around a black hole. I thought he was just raving, but when he sobered up he said the whole damned thing over again. Mentioned it the next night, got laughed at, and never talked about it again. Want to meet him?"

"Not especially," said Lane.

"That's why I love you, Nicobar." Tchaka laughed. "Always gracious. Hey, Mariner!" he shouted to the old man. "Come on over here and grab yourself a free drink, courtesy of Nicobar Lane."

The old man looked up, seemed to consider the offer, then arose painfully and hobbled over to the bar. He took the drink Tchaka offered him, downed it without a word or a breath, then wiped his mouth with a tattered sleeve. He had been strong and vigorous once, and even now he looked more pained than wasted.

"Thanks," he said at last, in a voice that seemed even older than the body that housed it.

"You're welcome," said Lane, leaning on the bar in the hope that the Mufti would get another glimpse of Tchaka's ear-lizard. "What's your name, old man?"

"I'm not really sure," said the man. "I've been called the Mariner for so long that I've forgotten what my real name is. I guess I must have one, though."

"Why do they call you the Mariner?" asked Lane.

"For the Ancient Mariner."

"I don't see the connection," said Lane.

"Water, water everywhere, nor any drop to drink," quoted the old man. "With me it was planets. Millions of worlds, green worlds, blue worlds, red ones, deserts and oceans and jungles and mountains so tall you couldn't see the tops even on a clear day. I've seen them all, opened up a goodly number of them for colonists. But I could never stay on one, not for more than a month or so. I always thought there'd be a prettier one circling around the next star, always had to go chasing after it. Planets everywhere, a billion worlds for the asking, and none of them for me. So I wound up here, too old and too broke and too sick to go back to any of the Edens I walked out on."

"The Mariner was the man who discovered Northpoint," said Tchaka, pouring the old man another glass.

"That's right," said the Mariner. "Seventy-two years ago. Not one of my greater achievements, I must admit. Named the planet. Named this town, too. I never realized just how well I had named it until I got stuck here."

"I'll bet you've seen a lot of things in your time," said Lane.

"That I have," said the Mariner.

"Ever see anything escape a black hole?"

The Mariner glared at Tchaka. "Is that why you called me over here. To poke fun at me?"

"When we're through talking, Nicobar and I are going to poke a little fun at some of my women," said Tchaka with a grin. "As for you, old man, no one wants to humiliate you. We just want you to talk to us."

"About black holes," said Lane.

The Mariner stared long and hard at them. Then he shrugged, held out his glass for a refill, and began speaking.

"It happened thirty-seven years ago. I was working for the government then, charting habitable planets. I had just left New Kenya, which turned out not to be so habitable after all. Not that it was my fault—I mean, what the hell does an explorer know about volcanoes and earthquakes? I think they lost about half a million people in that holocaust.

"Anyway, they wanted water worlds, Lord knows why, so I set out for the Terrazane sector, where I knew conditions were ripe for a lot of ocean worlds: a whole batch of stars in the G-2 to G-8 range. You ever been out that way, Lane?"

"No," said Lane.

"Lot of garbage out there," said the Mariner. "Dust clouds so thick they blot out the stars for hours at a time. Makes a man feel claustrophobic. Just a bunch of junk that never managed to get together to form stars. Some of it was hot, too, though most of it wasn't. Anyway, that's where I got my first glimpse of the Starduster."

"The Starduster?" repeated Lane.

"The Starduster, the Starduster!" snapped the Mariner. "That's what the hell we're talking about, isn't it? Damned hell-spawned thing that floats out there in the vacuum, living off the stellar dust between the stars. Eats it just like you or I eat a steak."

"What did it look like?" asked Lane.

"Not sure," said the old man. "I kept losing sight of it

because of all the damned dust. But I was able to track it with my sensors, and I began following it. Pure energy it was, and faster than most spaceships."

"Was any part of it in the infrared end of the spectrum?" asked Lane.

"Hell, I don't know," said the Mariner. "But every now and then I could see it shimmering out there ahead of me, so it couldn't have been all infrared." He paused, looking at his now-empty glass, and Tchaka filled it up again as Lane slapped some more currency down on the counter.

"Thanks," said the old man. "That was some critter, that Starduster. But big as it was, it was scared to death of me."

"That doesn't sound very likely, old man," said Tchaka.

"Maybe not," agreed the Mariner, "but it's true just the same."

"How do you know?" persisted Tchaka.

"I'm not sure. Intuition, maybe. Anyway, it tried hell-for-leather to get away from me—and me, I was just young and strong and stupid enough that I wanted to get a better look, so I followed it. It led me a merry chase, I can vouch for that. Three, four, five parsecs, maybe more. Then we came to the Terrazane hole—biggest black hole I've ever seen, almost sixty miles across, without a speck of dust or garbage anywhere near it—and damn me if the Starduster didn't make right for it."

"See, Nicobar, I told you it sounded like your story," said Tchaka.

"You ran into it too?" asked the Mariner.

"I don't know," said Lane. "Probably not. Go on with your story."

"Not much left to it," said the Mariner. "I got as close as I dared, then tracked it on my panel. The damned thing went right up to the hole and at the last second it scooted around it."

"Did you follow it after that?" asked Lane.

"I tried," said the Mariner. "But it was so far ahead of me that I couldn't catch up."

"Ever see it again?" asked Lane.

"I thought I did once," said the old man. "It was in the Canphor system, but whatever it was I saw got the hell out of there so fast I couldn't be sure. Interesting beast, the Starduster. Can't figure out how it breathes or what purpose it has for living. I'd like to find out, though. You going after it, Lane?"

"Not a chance," said Lane.

"Too bad," said the Mariner. "I'd have liked to come along."

"I thought you were too old to ship out," said Tchaka.

"Oh, I figure I'd die during the trip," said the Mariner. "But I always wanted to die in space anyway. Doesn't bother me at all. I've seen just about everything there is to see in one lifetime, done everything I ever wanted to do. What the hell do I want to die in some hotel bed in Hellhaven for? I never really got a good look at the Starduster. I'd much rather die trying to get a glimpse of it than sit around here waiting to keel over. Toss my body out into space, let it blow up and go into a million orbits around a million stars. Don't want to be buried on any planet, Tchaka; not even on yours."

"I wish I could accommodate you, old-timer," said Lane, "but I hunt animals, not myths."

"That's too bad, Lane. I could even have told you where to find it."

"And how could you do that, old man?" said Tchaka, a condescending smile on his huge, thick lips.

"It feeds, just like any other animal," said the Mariner. "Let me know where you saw it, we'll mark down where I saw it, we'll add the sightings of those fools who think it's the Dreamwish Beast, and we'll get some idea of its feeding patterns."

"*If* it eats interstellar dust," said Tchaka. "How do you know it wasn't just resting there when you found it?"

"It makes sense," interjected Lane. "Anything big enough to show up on the instrument panel of one of those little government ships they had thirty or forty years ago has to be pretty big, and it's got to expend a lot of energy to be able to outrun a spaceship. I imagine that it feeds ninety percent of the time, maybe more. And besides, if it's an energy form, it's not likely to land on any planets to eat something solid. I would have guessed it fed off solar energy, but I suppose that would make it too much like a cannibal. I don't know what nourishment it can get out of a dust cloud, but for the moment I'm willing to accept that it lives off of them."

"What happens when it runs out of dust?" asked Tchaka.

"Never will," said the Mariner. "God was a lousy craftsman. The whole universe is cluttered with His leftovers."

"It's an interesting animal," said Lane.

"Then why not go out after it?" said the Mariner.

"I'm a hunter," said Lane. "I kill things for money. If I don't get paid, I don't kill things. Nobody's going to pay me for killing your Starduster, or Dreamwish Beast, or whatever."

"Why not?" said Tchaka. "They come out here in bunches to pay you to do just that."

"No corpse," said Lane. "Even if I knew how to kill it, which I don't, I imagine its remains would immediately dissipate. No *corpus delicti*, no money. Museums can't display memories."

"Still, wouldn't you like to see it close up?" asked the Mariner. "I'd trade my life for one good look."

"That's because you don't have much life left to trade, old man." Tchaka laughed. "Nicobar, he's the cautious type. He wants to live to be as old as you."

"Where did you see it?" asked the Mariner.

"The Pinnipes system," said Lane.

"Didn't know they had a black hole out there," said the old man. He squeezed his eyes shut and lowered his head, lost in thought and computations. "It *could* be the Starduster," he said at last. "It just could be."

"No clouds nearby," said Lane.

"None that you could see," said the Mariner. "Maybe they were there anyway. Or maybe it eats other things too. But it could be the same creature. The last Dreamwish Beast sighting was in the Alphard system, you know."

"That's not that far away from Pinnipes," said Lane, staring at his glass.

"Just a hope, a skip, and a jump," agreed the Mariner. "Getting your interest up, Lane?"

"Not even a little bit," said Lane. "There's a lot of stars out there, and just one beast."

"We'll find him," said the Mariner.

"We won't even look for him," said Lane.

"What's the matter with you, Lane?" said the Mariner. "You been doing too much killing? Hell, you're deader than the corpses you bring in."

"What are you talking about, old man?" said Tchaka.

"I'm talking about the kind of a man who would rather kill sitting ducks than go out into the unknown and hunt down the Starduster. I'm so old I can't even stand up without an effort, but that's only on the outside. Inside I'm a damned sight younger than the butcher here."

Tchaka lowered his lids, watching Lane carefully out of both eyes—the normal and the unique—to see if there would be any reaction. But there wasn't. Lane just gazed calmly at the Mariner.

"Look at him," said the old man contemptuously. "Not a feeling in his body. He can't even get mad anymore. No, Lane, you're not the man to go out after the Starduster. All you want to do is live vicariously through Tchaka's whores and drugs and watered whiskey."

"I don't water anyone's whiskey!" said Tchaka with mock indignation. "Except yours, old man. If I gave it to you straight, the shock would kill you. Come to think of it, just about everything I peddle would kill you."

"What you peddle is for men like Lane," said the Mariner. "Men like me never needed that stuff, not when I was young and not now when I'm old. I've seen the flare of a star going supernova. I've stood on worlds where no man ever stood before. I've gone spearfishing in a chlorine sea and stood atop the tallest mountain in the galaxy. I've held a diamond the size of your phony eyeball in my hand, and threw it away because my pockets were loaded with bigger ones. I've seen creatures that spend their entire lives following the sunset around their planet, and I've seen beasties that smell colors and see noises. What can you offer me to equal that, Tchaka? A drunken slut, a drug that'll send me off to some brown-gray dreamworld that's not half so interesting as the dullest planet I've put down on? No, goldtooth, sell your wares to someone like Lane. Me, I'll take the Starduster."

"Are you going to just sit there and take this, Nicobar?" said Tchaka.

"Nope," said Lane, rising. "I'm ready for your back room now."

"Ahhh!" said Tchaka, a smile of anticipation making his features even more grotesque. He clapped his hands and gestured to five of his girls, who immediately went through a tasseled doorway behind the bar.

The Mariner began limping back to his table, body stooped but head erect, eyes unblinking and staring straight ahead of him.

"Mariner!" called Lane in a loud, clear voice.

The old man turned to him.

"Do you know where my hangar is?"

"I can find it."

"Be there two days from now with your gear."

"You're going after him?" said the Mariner, a tremor of excitement in his voice.

"No," said Lane. "But if you've got your heart set on dying in space, it might as well be aboard the *Deathmaker* as any other ship."

"Thank you, Lane."

"You're welcome, Mariner," said Lane. Then he turned and followed Tchaka into the next room.

CHAPTER
4

Lane was mildly surprised to discover that the Mariner wasn't a burden.

The old man knew his way around a spaceship. He also possessed a remarkable mind, filled to the brim with the trivia of a thousand planets, much of it quite useful to Lane in his pursuit of exotic life forms. He also knew how to skin a carcass as neatly as any Dabih, which meant that Lane was able to get by with a crew of two: himself and the Mariner.

Even the Mufti, who ordinarily tolerated no one but Lane, took a liking to the Mariner. The old man spent hours each day recalling past glories and adventures in the purplest of prose, and by the time he was done recounting the day's quota of stories the Mufti could usually be found curled up on his lap, purring gently and allowing the Mariner to scratch between what passed for its shoulderblades.

They made two short hunts, each of about three months' duration. Then Lane took an order for two dozen Horndemons, enormous omnivores with truly phenomenal antlers, from Ansard IV, a planet which was within half a parsec of the Pinnipes system.

"Now maybe we'll catch a glimpse of him," said the Mariner as the *Deathmaker* took off for Ansard.

"Mariner," said Lane, "even a patient man like me gets a little tired of hearing about the Starduster every other day for six months. Besides, it's been more than a year since I was at Pinnipes—and I still don't know for a fact that it wasn't an alien ship."

"Nonsense," said the Mariner. "We both know damned well what you saw. Are you afraid that if you admit it you'll have to hunt it down?"

"No," said Lane. "But it's a big galaxy. There's a lot of stuff out there. The odds that we both saw the same thing are pretty slim."

"You don't think God would make *two* creatures like that, do you, Lane? You saw the Starduster, all right. What I can't figure out is why you're so loath to acknowledge it."

"Maybe I just don't want to get interested in it," said Lane. "I can see spending a half century trying to hunt the damned thing down without ever getting within hailing distance of it. Besides, there's no money in it."

"Well," said the old man, "I suppose that's one way to fight temptation. Me, I'd rather look it right in the eye and stare it down."

"Just don't tempt me to grant you your last wish a little prematurely," said Lane.

"You're talking through your hat, Lane." The Mariner smiled. "Even having me irritate you about the Starduster is better than being bored to death all by yourself."

"Tell me, Mariner, does anyone else call it the Starduster?"

"Dunno," said the Mariner. "Probably not. It goes by a lot of names: the Dreamwish Beast, the Starduster, the Deathdealer, half a dozen more. Names don't matter. You know what it is. So do I. Starduster's as good a way of identifying it as any other."

"Why Deathdealer?" asked Lane. "Has it ever killed anyone?"

"Not to my knowledge," said the Mariner, "though if it has, I imagine nobody'd come back to tell the story."

"You know, my first ship was called the *Deathdealer*."

"Why not?" The old man shrugged. "A ship's name is just a way of announcing yourself. Hardly expect Nicobar Lane to scoot around the galaxy in something named the *Peacemaker*."

"That used to be the name of a gun, back when we were still Earthbound," said Lane. "They blew a lot of men apart with the Peacemaker."

"Contradiction in terms," said the Mariner. "Nobody ever made peace by killing each other. Of course, they may have temporarily made war unnecessary or impractical, but I don't see that as being quite the same thing. Peacemaker—hah! You got a lot of faults, Lane, but you're honest. I'll give you that. *Deathdealer* was the right name for your ship."

"Thanks a lot," said Lane dryly. "Getting back to the names: Why was it called the Dreamwish Beast? That's the name I hear most often."

"It's the most common one," agreed the Mariner. "But that doesn't necessarily make it the best one. Sounds pretty, kind of mystical. Still, there's nothing dreamlike or wishful about it. It's a stupid name."

"Just the same, it'd be interesting to know how the name came to be," said Lane.

The old man pressed his lips together and made an obscene sound. "Dumb name. Starduster, that's what it is."

"Have it your way, Mariner," said Lane. "Ready for some dinner?"

"Breakfast," corrected the old man. "And no, I'm not ready. Got some work to do."

"What?" asked Lane.

"Haven't plotted out the Starduster's feeding grounds yet," said the Mariner. "Ought to do it, so we'll know where to look."

"First of all, you've got almost two Standard months before we reach Ansard," said Lane. "And second, we're hunting for Horndemons, not the Starduster."

"If I can show you where it is . . ." began the old man.

"No," said Lane firmly. "Now, are you coming back to the galley to eat?"

"Later," said the Mariner, his hand working so swiftly on the Carto-System that his fingers became nothing more than a blur as they raced over keys, switches, and levers. Lane shook his head and walked to the galley to fix his dinner.

When Lane returned half an hour later the old man had thrown a new chart into the Carto-System, which now displayed a twelve-parsec section of the galaxy, encompassing Pinnipes, Terrazane, Canphor, and perhaps two dozen other stars and worlds around which the Starduster had been sighted during the past century.

"See the cloud?" said the Mariner, flicking a pair of switches that activated a glowing three-dimensional cloud of interstellar dust and debris. "It starts a parsec past Terrazane, winds in and out of the Canphor region, and up past Pinnipes."

"That's an awfully sweeping generalization, Mariner," said Lane, looking at the chart. "Hell, the cloud doesn't come anywhere near Canphor. And look here—it goes right past Alphard, and there's never been a sighting in that region."

"Who can say what its exact habits are, Lane?" said the Mariner. "All I know is that every sighting I've heard of has been within a parsec of the cloud, and usually a hell of a lot closer."

"Even if you were right," said Lane, "a fact I am granting solely for the sake of argument, that's still a mighty big dust cloud. You could spend ten lifetimes without covering more than a third of it. Don't forget: when we go at light speeds, or even near them, our sensors are just about as useless as our eyes. There's no way to conduct a thorough search even if you had a captain who was willing to hunt for it.''

''Don't have to,'' said the Mariner. ''Standing where you're at, his progress has always been from right to left. Now, Pinnipes isn't that far from the end of the cloud, so it stands to reason that he's somewhere between Pinnipes and—''

''What makes you think he hasn't doubled back?'' said Lane, interested in spite of himself. ''He's been around a long time, maybe longer than the whole race of man. It seems to me that he'd know the limitations of his pasture by now. Why mess around at the edges?''

''No,'' said the old man, shaking his head. ''He's got to be a creature of habit, Lane. He hasn't got any natural predators, so he can go wherever he wants. There's a pattern to things in the universe, a regularity that could only exist when Chance operates on this huge a scale. He'll feed down to the end of the cloud, then come back again.''

''*If* he exists, and *if* he eats the dust cloud,'' said Lane.

''He exists, all right, as sure as Satan sits on the throne of Hell,'' said the Mariner.

''Listen, Mariner,'' said Lane, ''we're going to be cooped up here for another fifty or sixty days. I'm going to expect a little variety in your conversational subject matter in the days to come, and if I don't get it, both of us are going into Deepsleep.''

''I'll make you a deal, Lane,'' said the Mariner after a short silence.

''What?''

''How long do you plan to take catching the Horndemons?''

''Five weeks, maybe six,'' said Lane.

''If I show you how to do it in less than a week, can we spend the other five weeks looking for the Starduster?''

"I've never even seen a Horndemon," said Lane, "but according to the data in my ship's computer, it's going to take more than a month just to hunt them down. They live in the thickest part of a rain forest. Also, we're going to have to pick them off one at a time; they take forever to die, and I don't need four or five wounded Horndemons ganging up on me at the same time."

"You didn't answer me," said the Mariner. "Is it a deal?"

"It can't be done."

"Then you've got nothing to lose, have you?" said the old man with the kind of smug smile that made Lane want to rearrange his face.

"Look, Mariner, according to the computer—"

"Lane, who the hell do you think charted the damned planet?" said the Mariner. "Everything your computer knows is based on my reports."

"Then you know something that wasn't in the reports?" said Lane.

"Of course I do," said the Mariner. "I made my reports for miners and colonists, not for hunters."

"Am I correct in assuming that you won't tell me what you know if I don't agree to your terms?"

"That's right, Lane."

Lane lowered his head in thought for a long minute. "All right, you old bastard," he said at last. "You've got yourself a deal. Now, how are you going to kill the Horndemons?"

"You'll see." The Mariner grinned. "In the meantime, I'd suggest you start thinking about how you're going to kill the Starduster. We can talk about it when I'm through with breakfast."

He rose and hobbled off to the galley, singing an old space chanty about a bald, green-skinned woman named Beela who had three of everything that might conceivably be considered important.

CHAPTER
5

Ansard IV was a hot planet, hot and humid. Almost three-quarters of it consisted of a blue-green freshwater ocean. The rest—one large continent and three island continents—consisted of primeval forests, dense jungles, a trio of awesome mountain ranges, and an occasional desert. The island continents had numerous inland lakes, as well as immense rain forests. The branches of these forests occasionally shut out the sunlight, but somehow the rain managed to get through even where the sunlight couldn't. It rained every minute of every day in portions of the forest, and enough rain fell in other sections so that the ground was usually submerged beneath a sea of mud and slop.

No one had yet bothered cataloguing the insect life of Ansard IV, but Lane estimated that the man who took on that particular job wouldn't be finished until well after he'd reached his two millionth species. The air wasn't quite as oxygen-rich as some jungle worlds he'd been on, but it was sufficient for him to take a depressant every three hours to make sure he kept his senses about him. He had set the *Deathmaker* down on a sandy ocean beach, as per the Mariner's instructions. Then he took samplings of the atmosphere, water, some simple specimens of the flora and fauna (i.e., grass and insects), and extracted the equipment he felt he'd need from his cargo hold. He deposited the Mufti in the Deepsleep machine and sought out the Mariner, who was walking around barefoot on the sand outside the ship, his boots in his hands.

"Well?" said Lane.

"Well what?" asked the old man.

"If you want to clear out of here in a week or so and go looking for your Starduster, I'd suggest you tell me how we plan to find and kill two dozen Horndemons."

"Easy," said the Mariner. "See that old volcano?" He pointed to a mountain about eight miles distant.

"Yes."

"That's where they are."

"On the slopes or inside it?" asked Lane.

"Inside it. Volcano hasn't gone off in eons. Its floor is covered with grasses and a couple of forests, and enough water so nothing inside it ever has to leave. Just like the Ngorongoro Crater back on Earth."

"We saw a lot of craters during our descent," said Lane. "How can you be sure that this is the one that contains the Horndemons?"

"This is the most convenient one to walk to," said the Mariner. "That's why I chose it. They're just about all the same. As for Horndemons—hell, there's nothing on this world can give them a tussle. They practically own the damned planet. They live in every forest, every jungle, and every crater."

"Why didn't you tell me to land in the crater?" said Lane. "This is a pretty versatile ship. I could have done it without much difficulty."

"And take a chance of scaring the critters away? Not a chance, Lane. If I can walk eight miles, so can you."

"I suppose you have no objection to my setting down in

the crater once we've killed the damned things," said Lane. "Or would you rather carry them back here?"

"I hadn't really thought of that," admitted the Mariner.

"Nor of how we're going to keep the insects away from the carcasses while we walk back to the ship?" said Lane. He smiled for an instant as the Mariner looked uncomfortable. "Don't worry, Mariner. I've got a preservative we can spray them with. It'll harden on contact and last long enough so that nothing will be able to eat through it before I return with the ship. It's a derivative of the stuff I use to preserve skins and carcasses in the cargo hold."

"What are you planning to kill them with?" asked the Mariner.

"A screecher," said Lane.

"They're pretty big animals," said the Mariner dubiously.

"I know," said Lane. "But they're for museums. I can't damage the hides. I'll take a molecular imploder along too, just in case I run into trouble. I'd rather not use it, though; it leaves a pretty sloppy corpse."

"You're the hunter." The old man shrugged.

"That I am," said Lane. "Feel up to setting out now, or would you rather wait until tomorrow?"

"The sooner we leave the sooner we'll get the job done with," said the Mariner.

They packed food and medical kits, Lane's weapons, the preservative, a compass, various stimulants and depressants, insect repellent, lanterns and beacons, and water, and began their trek through the primeval forest.

It was slow work, foot-slogging through the mud and climbing over the roots of trees that had to be millennia old. They rested frequently, mostly for the Mariner's sake, but proceeded at a steady rate of two miles per hour.

Lane was amazed by the variety in size and appearance of the various insects. There was one flying species in particular that fascinated him, a huge dragonfly-type that measured almost forty centimeters in length. They seemed to have no eyes, antennae, or other sensory organs, but they were death and taxes when it came to zeroing in on smaller insects. He couldn't even discern mouths on the things, nor was their method of attacking at all enlightening. They swooped down, picked the hapless prey up in powerful pincers, and flew off with it. Try as he would, Lane couldn't figure out how they ingested their food.

He asked the Mariner about them, but the old man just shook his head.

"They're either mutated or localized," he said. "At any rate, I didn't see them when I charted the planet. Maybe their mouths are in their pincers."

"Uh-uh. Too inefficient," said Lane. "The closest I can come to an explanation would be that they crush the smaller insects against their abdomens and feed by a form of osmosis, but it doesn't seem to me that they could get a hell of a lot of nourishment that way."

"Who knows?" The old man shrugged. "Kill a couple on the way back and dissect them. When you're through studying them you can always give 'em to the Mufti."

"He only likes live insects," said Lane. He looked around him. "He'd have a field day out here."

"Let's get to the crater before the damned insects figure out we're good to eat and start having a field day of their own," said the Mariner, increasing his pace.

They walked in silence for another thirty minutes. Then they heard a strange, hollow, hooting scream to the northwest, followed by the sound of branches breaking.

"A Horndemon?" asked Lane, his casual grip on the imploder suddenly becoming a very businesslike one.

"Too big and loud to be anything else," said the Mariner.

"Stick close by, Mariner," said Lane. "I don't imagine

we'll be coming to any clearings, so we're going to be running blind, for all practical purposes.''

"Don't go worrying about any surprise attacks," said the Mariner. "There's nothing going to sneak up on us without giving us plenty of warning. The forest is too dense for that.''

"I've already been warned," said Lane. "As for sneaking up on us, I don't imagine they have any intention of doing so. However, if you can tell me where the damned thing is going to jump us just from hearing a couple of branches break twenty yards away, I'd sure appreciate it if you'd share your knowledge with me. Also, I don't know for a fact that there's only one Horndemon out there. In fact, all the information you poured into the computer would lead me to think that a solitary Horndemon is pretty rare.''

"Well, it isn't going to be solitary for long if you keep talking," said the Mariner.

"It'll know we're here whether I talk to you or not," said Lane, his eyes scanning the bushes that surrounded him. "We make a lot of noise just traipsing through here, and I'm not about to stop and spend the night in this mire. Horndemons or not, I plan to camp on the rim of the crater tonight. This stuff's too hard to breathe, and I'd be a damned sight happier if I didn't have to pull insects out of my boots every couple of minutes.''

They continued walking, albeit more cautiously, and reached the base of the volcano without incident three hours later. The jungle thinned as they ascended it, and another four hours found them at the top, just as the huge sun was beginning its descent. They ate a sparse meal, then propped themselves up against a pair of smooth trees and fell asleep, weapons in hand.

Lane awoke with the sunrise, and saw a huge horned creature standing thirty yards away, regarding him curiously. It was reddish-brown in color, its hair wiry in texture. It had four legs, stood approximately the size of a small bison, and had a pair of horns that dwarfed even the legendary greater kudu of old Earth's African hills. It looked pretty innocuous, like just another species of herbivore, until he saw its feet. They were splayed, and seemed to have retractable claws. *That* smacked of a carnivore.

He studied its head, briefly but expertly. The eyes weren't wide-set, which meant that it's peripheral vision wasn't all that good. That, too, smacked of a carnivore. Still, the body was too large for a pure carnivore on this world; there simply weren't enough game animals to keep it fed. The shape of the jaws reflected this: totally unspecialized, not quite long enough to house the numerous grinding teeth of a pure herbivore, not hinged well enough for a pure carnivore. The ears were large, which seemed appropriate for a world where the jungles limited visibility so much. Right at the moment they were both pricked forward, pointing at Lane.

The Horndemon was staring at him with neither malice nor fear, which was to be expected of a beast that had no natural enemies and had never seen a man before. Lane laid the imploder across his lap and slowly picked up his screecher. Carefully, gently, making sure not to make any sudden movements, he aimed the screecher at the Horndemon and pressed the trigger mechanism.

The results were startling. The Horndemon did a complete backflip in the air, hit the ground with a resounding thud, shook its head vigorously, floundered once, and then began emitting the same hollow hooting noise Lane had heard the previous day. Suddenly its eyes fell on Lane again, and it staggered up and charged across the intervening ground with a swiftness that Lane hadn't expected in so large a creature. He dropped the screecher and picked up and fired the imploder all in one motion. The Horndemon gave one surprised grunt and turned to jelly in midcharge.

"I wasn't kidding when I said they were hard to kill," said the Mariner, still leaning against his tree.

"You were awake?" said Lane, startled by his voice.

"Yep. I just wanted to see what kind of hunter I'd hooked up with, so I kept quiet and watched."

"You've already been on two hunts with me," said Lane. "What did you plan to do if the damned thing charged while I was sleeping?"

"Shoot it with my own screecher," said the Mariner. "You'd have been awake before it got around to doing anything serious. By the way, why'd you kill it with the imploder? You could have jumped behind the tree and kept the screecher on."

"We couldn't have loaded this one into the ship," said Lane. "Even if the screecher killed it I'd have turned the imploder on the carcass."

"Tough bastards, aren't they?" said the Mariner, looking at what little remained of the Horndemon.

"Yes, they are," said Lane. "I've had creatures survive the screecher for a while, but they've always tried to run away from it. This is the first time I ever saw an animal run right into the sound waves that are scrambling his brain. I don't think he was disoriented, either; just mean and tough. I don't see being able to kill one with a screecher in much less than a minute, and probably it'll go closer to ninety seconds. That means I'll have to get within about seventy-five yards. Any closer and I might have to use the imploder if it charges; much farther and it could run out of the screecher's effective range."

"Beautiful things, screechers," said the old man. "Stand in front of one and it burns out half your brain circuits; fire it and you don't even hear a hum."

"The Horndemon didn't hear anything either. He just felt it." Lane stood up, picked up his gear, took one last look at the remains of the Horndemon, and turned to the Mariner. "We might as well get started. The next Horndemon I kill I want to take back with me."

They reached the floor of the crater in less than five hours. Then, with between eight and nine hours of sunlight left, the hunt began in earnest.

Lane found his first Horndemons in a grove of fruit trees about four hundred meters from the crater wall. It took him almost an hour to isolate one of them from its four companions, but he finally accomplished it and fired the screecher at a distance of eighty yards. This Horndemon reacted even more violently than the one on the rim had done; finally it saw Lane and raced toward him, collapsing less than the length of its body from Lane's feet.

Lane immediately turned to look at the other four. Two had fled into the denser forest behind the grove, one was staring at him, and one was approaching. He debated killing the nearer one with the imploder and going after the second one with the screecher, but decided to see if he could keep both of them intact. He dispatched the nearer of the Horndemons without much difficulty, and still the other made no motion.

"It's like shooting fish in a barrel, to borrow an old expression," said Lane to the Mariner, who was standing a short distance behind him. "No one has ever hunted them before; they don't know enough to be scared."

He walked toward the remaining Horndemon. He was just about to aim the screecher when the creature charged down upon him without a sound. Lane was surprised but unexcited. He took careful aim and fired the screecher at thirty yards. The Horndemon fell to its knees for an instant, but almost immediately regained its feet. Lane kept the screecher trained on it. The Horndemon kept coming, but was staggering now, and Lane jumped nimbly aside at the last instant. Then the beast's eyes fell on the Mariner, and it lowered its horns and charged the old man.

Lane dropped the screecher and fired the imploder. The beast was so close to the Mariner when it died that Lane had to help him out from under what remained of it.

"Thanks, Lane," said the Mariner, gasping for breath.

"Go to hell, old man!" snapped Lane. "From now on *you* hold the imploder and keep at least a hundred yards behind me. And God help you if we have to turn another Horndemon into putty."

He went back to the two usable corpses and applied the preservative. This done, he walked over to the remains of the third carcass and had the Mariner use the imploder on it again, until nothing but liquid remained. Lane stood there until it had all seeped into the soft ground.

"What was that for?" asked the Mariner.

"The Horndemons don't know that another predator has set up housekeeping here," said Lane. "Why leave any hints?"

"What about the other two carcasses?"

"The preservative will kill any odor, and from the way these creatures are built, I'd guess they'll believe their noses before their eyes."

Lane killed three more Horndemons in late afternoon, then set up camp at the base of the crater wall, surrounding the area with a number of warning devices. None were triggered, and the next day he killed seven more of the beasts.

By the third day they had become more cautious, and he changed his base of operations, moving to the far side of the crater, some nine miles distant. Here he downed eight more Horndemons in the next two days before he found it expedient to move again.

By the morning of the sixth day he had filled his order, and, hardly feeling like a heroic hunter, he returned to the *Deathmaker*, awoke the Mufti, picked up his Horndemons, and prepared himself for an uneventful six weeks in space while the Mariner chased after his elusive dream.

CHAPTER
6

A week passed. Then another, and a third.

The *Deathmaker* had passed Pinnipes, gone to the end of the dust cloud, and begun its trek back. There was no sign of the Starduster.

The ship passed half a dozen stars, then twenty more. It shot in and out of the cloud, it sought out the few charted black holes, it set off an occasional flare. There was no response.

"Looking for a needle in a haystack would be easy compared to this," said Lane as the two of them were relaxing over a meal. "It's a damned big galaxy, Mariner, and a damned small beast."

"He's around somewhere," said the Mariner with conviction. "I'm an old, crippled man, Lane, and that bit of mountain climbing on Ansard IV didn't do me any good. But if there's a God anywhere in the cosmos, He's not going to let me die without getting a good close look at the Starduster. I've been too many places, seen too many strange things, to not be vouchsafed another look at the strangest thing of all."

"First we've got to find it," said Lane. "Then you can look to your heart's content."

"We'll find him, all right," said the Mariner.

"You've got three weeks left," said Lane, rising from the table and walking over to his hammock.

It didn't take three weeks, or even two. It took precisely eleven days, two hours and thirty-five minutes.

"Well, I'll be damned," said Lane, scanning his instrument panel. "Either there's a ship out there going no place in particular, or else we've caught up to your Starduster after all."

He stepped aside and let the old man look at the panel. The Mariner tried a spectroscopic analysis and came up with a blank.

"It's him, all right," he said, his eyes alight with excitement. "Pure energy, and damned near as big as a neutron star."

"You didn't get that description from our sensing equipment," said Lane.

"He's a giant, that one," said the Mariner. "Get close enough and he'll blot out the stars."

"A little less bad poetry and a little more navigation," said Lane, having the computer plot a pair of courses that would allow the *Deathmaker* to intersect the creature's path and choosing the less direct one.

Lane tracked the creature on his panel while the *Deathmaker* began eating up the distance between them. It was moving along in an unhurried fashion, very much like the last time he had seen it. They were still about two hours from the intersection point when the creature changed its course.

"Think he's trying to get away from us, Lane?" asked the Mariner.

"I doubt it," said Lane. "It probably doesn't even know we're here yet. Besides, why should it try to evade us?"

"Maybe he knows we've got a killer on board," said the Mariner.

"Let's not endow it with too many paranormal abilities just yet," said Lane. "Besides, we just want to look at it, not kill it."

"Maybe he doesn't know the difference," said the Mariner. "And once we get close enough, maybe you won't know the difference either."

"I don't mind the fact that you borrowed your name from the Ancient Mariner," said Lane, "but I sure as hell wish you wouldn't try so hard to sound like him." He turned back to the computer, fed in the creature's new coordinates, and changed the ship's course accordingly.

Another ninety minutes passed uneventfully, and then Lane activated the ship's viewing screens.

"If it'll just get out of the cloud for a minute, we ought to be able to see it," said Lane. "From this distance it'll probably look like a very bright star, but it ought to be pulsating a bit and moving like all hell."

They waited, their eyes shifting from the panel to the screen and back again, but the creature showed no inclination to leave the dust cloud.

"We're getting close now," said Lane at last. "Maybe we can scare it out of there."

He took over manual control of the *Deathmaker* and got to within about eight thousand miles. The creature still remained within the cloud, and he fired one of his laser cannons.

"Don't kill it before I get to see it!" yelled the Mariner.

"It's going to take something more than a laser to kill that thing," said Lane. "I'm just trying to prod it out into the open."

The creature came to a complete stop, and Lane found himself within a thousand miles before he could bring the *Deathmaker* to a halt. He could see just the hint of the Starduster now, a section of the cloud that seemed to glow faintly.

"I don't like this," said Lane. "The damned animal ought to be doing *something*."

He began moving in again, stopping at five hundred yards. His hands were moist, and his left eyelid began to itch. He inched the ship forward.

"Damn it!" he muttered. "Why doesn't it move?"

"You're shaking like a leaf, Lane," said the Mariner with a hysterical laugh.

"You don't look all that relaxed yourself," shot back Lane, looking at the sweat-drenched old man.

They remained thus, motionless, spaceship and space beast. Lane suddenly became aware of the fact that he was indeed trembling, just as the Mariner had said. It upset him. In a quarter century of hunting and killing he had been in his share of tight scrapes, and usually he became calmer as the situation grew more tense. Now he found himself fighting a blind panic deep within himself, an urge to turn tail and run as quickly as possible.

With an enormous effort of will he forced his hand back to the acceleration controls and began approaching the creature once again. The Mariner strapped himself into a chair and pressed hard against its back, his face ashen, his hands in a deathgrip on the chair's arms.

The creature began retreating, and finally burst from the cloud into open space. The *Deathmaker* followed it a few seconds later, and the two men got their first good look at it. It was shaped like an irregular sphere, glowing a dullish red-orange and constantly fluctuating in intensity. There seemed to be no sensory organs and no means of motive power, though it was obvious that the creature was completely aware of its surroundings and quite capable of leaving them at will. It was large, perhaps seven miles in diameter, although its dimensions changed minutely with each fluctuation in its color. Lane couldn't even begin to guess how it ate, what it ate, how it reproduced, or even *if* it reproduced. He suspected that it didn't. It could have been a year old, or a century, or as old as the galaxy; there was a timelessness about it that made such speculation seem both futile and unnecessary. It hung in space, an enormous, pulsating, living thing of pure energy, awesome in its size and the potential of its power.

"Well," said Lane, "was it worth waiting for?"

"Magnificent!" whispered the Mariner. "He's everything I knew he'd be."

"Let's see if we can't make it jump a little bit and figure out how it moves," said Lane.

He turned the ship's molecular imploder on the creature, but it had no visible effect.

"Figures," muttered Lane. "The damned thing hasn't got any molecules."

He still had an occasional frenzied impulse to flee, but he found it easier to control himself, now that the creature was drifting a little farther away.

"What's he doing out there, Lane?" asked the Mariner.

"Damned if I know," said Lane. "Sizing us up, probably; just what we're doing to it. It's beautiful, isn't it?"

They both looked at the creature in the viewscreen—and as they did so, it stopped drifting away and began approaching them.

"Two choices," said Lane with a coolness he didn't feel. "We can run, or we can see if the vibrator will keep it at arm's length."

"Let's run," said the Mariner.

Lane wanted to run, too, wanted to run so badly that he forced himself to stay. He wasn't ussed to fear, was greatly troubled by it, and decided the only way to conquer it was to meet it head-on. He wasn't even thinking about the creature approaching the ship. His sole concern was defeating the secret demon that had suddenly been unleashed inside himself.

He moved his hand to the vibrator—a radio-frequency ship-size screecher—and fired a blast into the creature.

Then all hell broke loose.

Lane and the Mariner screamed simultaneously. The old man collapsed in a heap, but Lane managed to keep his balance if not his senses. All the fear and apprehension he had felt vanished, to be replaced with something else, something strange and alien and painful that threatened to tear his consciousness to pieces.

Solely from instinct he kept the vibrator trained on the creature and maneuvered the ship back into the dust cloud. Then he stood, motionless and unblinking, for the better part of ten minutes before his faculties returned to him.

He checked the viewscreen, but saw nothing except dust. The sensor panel couldn't come up with anything at first, but finally pinpointed an object that had to be the creature, racing away at near-light speed.

"Wake up, Mariner," said Lane, walking over to the old man and shaking him.

There was no response.

He put his head to the Mariner's chest, trying to find a heartbeat. There wasn't any.

He opened the old man's eyes. The pupils didn't respond to light. There was no pulse, no sign of breathing.

"Well, at least you saw it before you died," said Lane. He lifted the corpse over his shoulder, walked to an airlock, and deposited the body there. A moment later it was floating through space, a deformed hulk that had once been a man.

He shook his head, still dazed by whatever it was that had affected him. Then he went back to his panel, located the fleeing creature, and computed two courses—one in pursuit of the creature, and one to Northpoint.

He stared at them for a long time. Then, finally, he laid in the course for home, while deep inside him, almost unnoticed, a tiny voice screamed in agony and outrage.

CHAPTER
7

"Impossible!" said Tchaka.

"Why?" demanded Lane. "Because you never saw one before?"

"Because *nobody* ever saw one before!" said Tchaka.

They were sitting, drinks in hand, in Tchaka's chart shop. Covering every wall were maps of Northpoint, Northpoint's solar system, the galaxy, and a score of rarely seen worlds, some of them still thought to be figments of the cartographers' imaginations. One counter, looking like a huge wine rack, was filled with row upon row of rolled maps and charts, while all across the enormous chamber were bookcases and tapeholders stocked with ancient and semi-ancient maps. Hanging down in the center of the room was a large, meticulously detailed chandelier with hundreds of exact topographical representations of Earth and other human abodes. Numerous other globes, some hard and metallic, some shiny and sparkling like Tchaka's left eye, and a few made of materials entirely unknown to Lane, were placed artistically throughout the room.

"But we know empaths exist!" said Lane.

"No one has ever reported a *sending* empath before,"

said Tchaka. "Every race of empaths we've run across just receives."

"Well, maybe empath is the wrong word, then," said Lane. "But I'm telling you, Tchaka the damned thing sends out its own emotional impulses. Whenever I got too near it I was so scared I actually trembled."

"I would have been scared, too," said Tchaka. "So what?"

"Dammit, you don't understand!" snapped Lane. "I've never felt like that in my life."

"You never saw anything like the Dreamwish Beast in your life," said Tchaka.

"That has nothing to do with it. Hell, when I hunt Baffle-divers I use myself for bait in an ocean where the visibility is just about nil. That doesn't frighten me. More than once I've been ripped up by animals on unpopulated worlds with no one around to help me, and that never frightened me. But suddenly here I was, armed to the teeth in the *Deathmaker*, and I started shaking like a leaf."

"Different things scare different people," said Tchaka.

"Nothing scared me," said Lane. "But *I* scared *it*, and it radiated its fear to me. Whenever it got far enough away for some of the tension it felt to dissipate, so did mine."

"It seems to me, Nicobar," said Tchaka, absently scratching his artificial eyeball with the instrument he had been using to stir his drink, "that this is the most complicated rationalization for feeling afraid that I have ever heard in my life, long and filled with fascinating rationalizations as it has been."

"Thank you for your confidence," said Lane dryly.

"Anything for a paying customer," said Tchaka with a grin. "By the way, did you feel pain when you shot the beast, Nicobar? I assume you *did* shoot it."

"I used a vibrator on it."

"Then what are you doing here?" said Tchaka triumphantly. "If your theory is right, you should have died the second the beam hit the thing."

"It doesn't affect my theory at all," said Lane. "I don't think the Starduster, or Deathdealer, or whatever we're calling it, feels pain. At least, not like you and I do. I suppose, in retrospect, that it's not too surprising. Why would something composed of pure energy have sensations of pain?"

"Then it can't be killed?"

"I didn't say that," said Lane. "It can be killed, all right—and with a vibrator."

"But I thought you said—"

"That it didn't feel pain," said Lane. "That's a whole lot different from saying that it can't be killed."

"Not to me it isn't," said Tchaka.

"I tried the laser cannon on the creature, and the molecular imploder too," said Lane. "No effect. But I got a reaction with the vibrator."

"But not a pain reaction," said Tchaka.

"No."

"Then what kind of reaction was it?"

"A whole bunch of things, some of them too strange to understand, some too vague to clarify. The overwhelming impression I've been able to reconstruct has been one of great regret, with a goodly chunk of fear of the unknown mixed in."

"Could be anything," said Tchaka.

"No," said Lane. "It was something very specific. It was death."

"But you didn't kill it."

"I must have destroyed a tiny part of it, a minuscule portion of the totality. Enough to make the creature give me just a little taste of death."

"If you say so, Nicobar," said Tchaka. "But why did it kill only the Mariner and not you too?"

"Simple," said Lane. "The Mariner was an old man, ready to die, maybe even eager to do so after finally seeing his Starduster. I'm younger and stronger. I don't want to die yet. Maybe it takes more than a taste of death to kill me."

"Give my liquor a chance," said Tchaka, rising and walking to a bar that was hidden behind the chart rack. "It'll kill you before you ever see the Dreamwish Beast again. Besides, I still say there's no such thing as an emotional sending machine."

"Maybe not," said Lane. "Maybe it receives my emotions, too. There's no way for me to know that. But I know what I felt, and I know what killed the old man. I'd never had a nightmare in my life, but I've been having them every time I go to sleep since I ran into that creature."

"It must be quite a beast to give the great Nicobar Lane nightmares," said Tchaka, pouring himself another drink.

"It is. It's got one hell of a protective device," said Lane. "The more severely it's menaced, the more terror its attacker feels."

"Outside of you, Nicobar, who or what in the universe would attack it?"

Lane shrugged. "Something must, or it wouldn't have developed any defense mechanisms at all."

"That's the problem with you, Nicobar," said Tchaka, his gold teeth glinting in the chandelier's light as he allowed himself the luxury of a huge grin. "You view everything through the eyes of a hunter. Maybe there's more than just meat and meat-eaters in the universe."

"Such as?"

"Maybe God isn't a hunter, Nicobar. Maybe He's a lover."

"I haven't the slightest notion what you're talking about," said Lane.

"That mechanism, *if* it exists, is a very interesting thing to have. I ask myself: What would Tchaka do with it? And, since Tchaka is nothing if not kind, considerate, generous to a fault, and one hell of a stud to boot, I think I'd let women feel what I feel when I look at them, when I touch and fondle them, when I spurt my seed into them. That's the way I'd use it, Nicobar, and who's to say you're any closer to God's idea of the Dreamwish Beast than I am? Maybe it's a mating mechanism, Nicobar. Maybe it emotes lust and desire to attract other Dreamwish Beasts."

"You're going on the assumption that there *are* other Dreamwish Beasts," said Lane. "I'm not so sure about that."

"Maybe there aren't," said Tchaka. "But there are no natural enemies, either. Why should you think that this mechanism was created for one thing rather than the other?"

"If it's a mating mechanism, why would it also be able to broadcast terror, or death?" said Lane.

"Wouldn't you want a woman to tell you if you were killing her with pleasure?" Tchaka grinned. "But maybe I'm wrong. Maybe only Tchaka can send them to heaven that way."

"I thought all your women went to hell," said Lane.

"That's where they get their training, Nicobar," said Tchaka. "Once they've learned their trade, they come to work for me."

"I have no empirical evidence to the contrary," said Lane wryly.

"Let's go hunting for a little evidence," said Tchaka, preparing to leave the room.

"Tchaka," said Lane, "I've been to Earth once, and I've seen men and beasts on quite a few other worlds, but you are without question the only living entity I've ever found that is all appetite."

"It beats the hell out of chasing another spoonful of death." Tchaka laughed. "Put the question to me, and I'll choose life every time."

"Some people might disagree with your definition of life."

"What do they know?" scoffed Tchaka. "People who know how to live do it, Nicobar. People who don't know, define it."

"Have you ever thought of writing a book composed of your homely little philosophies?" said Lane with a smile.

"Often," said Tchaka. "But I have no respect for anyone who has time to read it."

"I suppose that makes a certain kind of sense," said Lane.

"Of course it does. I'm nothing if not sensible—except lecherous. Let's go back downstairs, Nicobar."

"No, thanks. I came up here for a reason."

"Other than speaking to Tchaka? My feelings are wounded."

"A little opium or a little blonde and they'll recover just fine," said Lane. "Somehow, Tchaka, I have difficulty viewing you as an object of sympathy."

Tchaka shrugged. "So what did you come up here for?"

"Why would anyone come up here? To look at maps."

"But they're all ancient and outdated," said Tchaka. "The only people who buy them are collectors."

"I know what they are."

"Then why waste your time with them?" said Tchaka. "Use one of them to find a water world and you'll wind up on a gas giant."

"I'm not looking for planets," said Lane, walking over to the chart rack and pulling a few maps out at random.

"Stars? What can you hunt on a star?"

"I'm not looking for stars, either," said Lane.

"Then what else is—?" Tchaka gave vent to a huge belly laugh. "You're looking for the Dreamwish Beast! It must have scrambled your brain, Nicobar; you won't find it on any maps!"

Lane looked up at the huge man. "Somebody who didn't know what it was could have listed it as a star. In the early days they didn't have our sophisticated sensing devices. Seen through a porthole or viewing screen, and partially obscured by the dust cloud, it could have looked like a distant star. If I can find a few such sightings, I can trace its feeding pattern even better.''

"But what difference does it make?" said Tchaka. "You're not going to go out after it."

"Call it curiosity," said Lane, looking at the first of the charts, then replacing it in the rack.

"I'll call it idiocy," said Tchaka as Lane unrolled another map. "The more you hurt it, the more it'll hurt you right back."

"I don't want to hurt it," said Lane. "I just want to learn a little more about it."

"That's what they all tell me when they go into the drug den," said Tchaka. "That thing is death, Nicobar. Come downstairs with me and sample some of the joys of life."

"Later," said Lane, looking at another map.

"Come on, Nicobar. It'll be on the house."

"Not now."

"Bah! Why do I give a damn?" shouted Tchaka. "I've never met any man I had less in common with. Why should I care what you do?"

"You shouldn't."

"What would you do if I picked you up and carried you downstairs?" said Tchaka.

"I'd probably try to kill you," said Lane.

"You couldn't do it, Nicobar."

"I suppose not. Are you going to try?"

"If I did, we wouldn't be friends anymore, would we?"

"No, we wouldn't," said Lane.

"Why should Tchaka care if you're his friend or not?"

"Opposites attract," said Lane with a smile.

"Maybe that's why you're so interested in the Dreamwish Beast," said Tchaka. "You can't get much more opposite than that."

"There is a difference between attraction and interest that seems to escape you," said Lane. "You are attracted to your whores. I am interested in the creature."

"Seems like a waste," said Tchaka. "The damned thing hasn't got any value any longer, now that you know what it's made of."

"Hardly as wasteful as a proprietor sampling his stock more often than his customers do," said Lane, pulling out another batch of charts. "The creature never had a value; your girls used to, before you used them up."

"Are you insulting my whores?" demanded Tchaka.

"Perish the thought," said Lane. "Only your integrity."

"In that case, you're forgiven," said Tchaka with a laugh. He walked to the door. "I'll send up a girl with some liquor for you."

"Not soon," said Lane, spreading charts across the beautifully woven rug. "And make it coffee."

"I weep for you, Nicobar," said Tchaka.

"I weep for whoever you're going to bed with tonight." Lane grinned.

"Shall I have her send up a glowing testimonial in the morning?" asked Tchaka, but Lane, completely engrossed as he pored over an ancient starmap, did not answer.

CHAPTER
8

He was three months out of Hellhaven, and his cargo hold

was filled almost to the bursting point.

He was three months out of Hellhaven, and his cargo hold
was filled almost to the bursting point.

It had been a good hunt. Birds, mammals, reptiles, amphib-
ians, marsupials, fish, and a pair of creatures that simply
couldn't be classified, all had fallen before his weaponry and
his skill.

Now, weary at last of slaughter, he sat at the navigational
computer of his ship, knowing full well that he had killed his
quota and filled his orders and should return to his home base,
and knowing full well that he wasn't going home at all.

He put the dust cloud on the Carto-System, then added all
the previous sightings of the Starduster, including the half-
dozen he had found on Tchaka's old star charts. Then he
varied the intensity of the tiny pinpricks of light that denoted
the sightings, making the more recent ones shine even
brighter. He had the *Deathmaker*'s master computer estimate
the creature's speed and probable course, had the Carto-
System zero in on the area, and laid in a course for it.

It was foolish. He admitted it to himself with the brutal
honesty that always characterized his self-appraisals. He
didn't have that much fuel left, and he'd probably have to set
down for more water if he didn't go straight back to North-

point right now. Traversing interstellar space didn't take much out of his ship or his wallet; landing and taking off did. And yet, he was within a week's flight of where the creature figured to be. It was too good an opportunity to pass by.

He took a Deepsleep for six days, leaving the Mufti to fend for itself. When he awoke he made a few minor course corrections, ate a huge meal—Deepsleep only slowed the metabolism to a crawl, rather than stopping it, and he always woke up famished—and began examining his various instrument panels. He did not find what he was looking for.

He spent the next two weeks in the vicinity, ducking into and out of the dust cloud without ever coming across any intimation of the creature. He remained there until the last possible moment, then made for Belial, a tiny planet possessing two Tradertowns and not much else.

Upon arriving, he left the *Deathmaker* in a spaceport hangar, put the Mufti in Deepsleep, and walked to the Palace, a rather rundown counterpart to Tchaka's. He ordered a veal-like dish for dinner, topped it off with two glasses of Alphard brandy, toyed with spending an hour or so in the whorehouse but decided against it, and rented a small room for the night.

When he awoke he paid his bill, asked at the desk if there were any antiquarian book/tape shops on Belial, managed to keep his temper as the clerk doubled over with laughter, and then walked back to the hangar.

"Almost ready?" he asked the chief of the service division.

"Yeah," said the man. "You didn't say how much fuel you wanted. There's been a strike recently, and prices are a little inflated in these parts, so all I gave you was enough to get home safely. I assume from your ship's registration papers that you're from Northpoint."

Lane nodded.

"Couldn't help looking in the hold when I was cleaning up the ship. You a hunter or something?"

"Yes," said Lane.

"That's some haul," said the man admiringly. "You must be pretty good at your trade."

"The best," said Lane without humor. "By the way, I want all the fuel you can give me. Ditto for drinking water."

"That's gonna cost you, Mr. Lane," said the man. "Like I said, the price of fuel is—"

"I know what you said," said Lane. "I've got an account at the big bank at Alphard and another one at Northpoint. Check them out if you have any problems."

"If I'm not sticking my nose in where it doesn't belong, Mr. Lane," said the man, "just what the devil are you going to hunt that will require all that fuel and still fit in what little cargo area you've got left?"

"Right the first time," said Lane.

"Huh?"

"You're sticking your nose in where it doesn't belong."

The man just stared at him for a long moment, then relayed the order to his work crew.

Lane took off that afternoon and headed back toward the dust cloud. He arrived three days later.

There was still no trace of the creature.

It didn't bother Lane that much. He enjoyed sitting alone at the controls of the *Deathmaker*, found it much more exhilarating than hunting down alien animals on alien worlds. In the days when the race was still Earthbound, hunters had extolled the virtues of feeling the wind or the salt spray of the sea in their faces, the sun on their shoulders, the intoxication of cool fresh air in their lungs. Lane felt sorry for them. He'd felt not just one sun on his neck and shoulders, but almost five hundred of them, had breathed cool clear air on a score of worlds and been on hundreds of worlds where a single breath of unfiltered air would have been instantly fatal, had been above and beneath not just saltwater oceans, but oceans of chlorine, ammonia, and half a dozen other noxious liquids. There was no romance to pitting oneself against the elements; it was a game, a deadly gamble with Nature, that every hunter sooner or later was doomed to lose. He looked through one of his viewscreens at a myriad of stars, his vision unobstructed by atmosphere or the grim knowledge that the stars were forever beyond his grasp, and wondered what the ancient hunters would feel if they could sit beside him for a few minutes.

He took the Mufti out of Deepsleep, fed it a handful of dead, dried-up lizards, then allowed it to sit on his lap as he whipped up a snack and returned to the controls. He leaned back in his chair, wedged one foot against the side of the navigational computer, crossed the other over it, and closed his eyes, absently stroking the Mufti's chest and neck with his left hand. A moment later he was asleep.

The next ten weeks passed uneventfully, and yet he was not discontented. He followed a plain routine: eating, exercising, caring for the Mufti, making sure nothing was rotting in the cargo hold, plotting course corrections, sleeping.

When he began to get too bored he took mild narcotics and hallucinogens, and once or twice he drank himself into a stupor. For the most part, though, he remained awake, calm, sober, clear-headed, and—the prime quality in a hunter—patient.

The nightmares remained with him, though he had gotten used to them and paid them no more attention than he would pay to any other irritant. Many times he would wake up screaming and trembling, only to become aware of his surroundings and slowly relax, finally going back to sleep.

Which is exactly what happened to him ten weeks out from Belial. He woke with a cry and lay in his hammock, shaking so badly that he almost capsized it. Finally his head cleared and he realized that he was within the confines of the *Death-maker*, and that he had been having a nightmare.

But this time the terror didn't leave him. It covered him like a blanket, real and oppressive. He felt a sweet salty taste in his mouth and realized that he had bitten halfway through his lower lip. He shook his head, trying to clear it—and with a cry of elation that somehow worked its way up through layer upon layer of fear, he understood what had happened.

Jumping out of the hammock, he ran to the main viewing screen—and saw the creature, hovering about three thousand miles away.

He put the ship on manual control and edged forward, simultaneously locking the vibrator's sights onto the Starduster. The creature backed away, and the *Deathmaker* increased its pace.

They moved through the cloud together for hours, separated by the same three thousand miles, and bit by bit the terror began to disappear. After half a day the creature was totally unafraid of Lane, and he took that opportunity to move in closer.

At one thousand miles he began to feel the creature's apprehension again, and by the time he was within three hundred miles he was more frightened than he had ever been in his life. He took his eyes from the screen and the panel long enough to look at the Mufti, which seemed totally unaffected, reinforcing his conclusion that the little animal was either unintelligent or else mad as a hatter.

He turned all of his sensing devices onto the creature again, trying to learn something more about its makeup. It was no use. Possibly it was intelligent, possibly not. Perhaps it had the analog to a flesh-and-blood being's internal organs, perhaps it didn't. Conceivably it had some special mechanism by which it moved through space, conceivably it had none. The sensors were totally useless.

Lane aimed his laser cannon about twelve degrees of arc above the creature and fired it. The Starduster felt no greater apprehension or fear, and didn't alter its course. Lane fired another beam, kept the cannon on, and lowered the beam until it pierced right through the center of the creature. There was no response.

He increased the *Deathmaker*'s speed, and the creature did likewise, so quickly that he made up only about one hundred yards, which led him to the tentative conclusion that it might very well be a two-way empath.

He moved his hand to the vibrator. If the creature could read his mind, or even his emotions, it should be increasing its speed now—but it did no such thing, and he was forced to rethink his analysis of it.

Of course, he reasoned, he'd had no intention of setting off the vibrator, and perhaps the creature knew it. The only way to find out whether it could anticipate his actions was to actually open fire.

A little thrill of excitement surged through him as he realized that of course this was what he had to do. He strapped himself into his seat, debated whether to make some protective arrangement for the Mufti, decided not to, and pressed the firing mechanism.

The feeling was as intense as the first time he had fired on the creature, months before. An emotional wave struck him with the power of a thunderbolt, jerked his head back, sent spasmodic tremors through his limbs. There was remorse, and an almost religious fear of the unknown, and something that might be a pain analog, and other things, deep and dark and mysterious and totally alien. Almost as strong, though not quite, was the feeling of shock and surprise.

He took his hand off the firing mechanism almost instantly and remained rigid, panting, glassy-eyed. When at last he gathered his senses about him the Starduster had vanished, but he found it on his panel and began tracking it again. As he did so, he began taking a mental inventory of his body: his heartbeat was returning to normal, the twitching and jerking of his muscles had almost ceased, his vision was still somewhat impaired but functional, his breathing remained slightly irregular, his associative powers seemed unimpaired.

Then he checked out the Starduster's readings. There was no way to measure its mass, but its volume seemed constant, and certainly there was no diminishing of its speed.

He spent four days in all-out pursuit without appreciably closing the gap between them. During that time the Mufti seemed to crave more affection and attention than usual, and he concluded that it must have felt something, however mild, when he had fired on the Starduster.

Lane ate nothing at all, slept only fitfully, and spent almost every waking moment with his eyes glued to the panel. He was almost five million miles behind the creature, which seemed to feel that this was a safe margin, for though he was sure it could have pulled even farther ahead of him it made no effort to do so.

It was harder and harder to keep track of the Starduster on his panel, which simply wasn't designed for this kind of work at greater-than-light speeds, and, on the fifth day of the chase, he lost all trace of it.

He spent the next three months trying to find it again. His mood ranged from black to blacker, and even the Mufti gave him a wide berth after the fourth week. Finally a couple of the carcasses began disintegrating, and he realized that he'd have to put in to a port very soon or risk losing his income from the entire hunt.

He lingered another day or two, hoping against hope that he might chance across the creature again, but at last he laid in a course for Lodin XI, the largest shipping world in the vicinity.

As the Lodin system came into view he was still thinking about the Starduster. He'd gotten closer to it this time, so close he could almost have reached out and touched it. And yet all he had received for his time and his trouble was another tiny taste of death, a sharing of something so strange and grotesque and eerie that no rational man would ever want to experience it again. Not Tchaka, with his exuberant lust for life; not the Mariner, with his yearning for the unknown; not Lane, with his emotions wiped clean after a quarter century of bloodletting.

And yet he had spent three months in pursuit of the strange, flowing, pulsating creature. He was still asking himself why as his ship passed by the orbiting fuel and shipping docks and prepared to set down on the dry, arid surface of Lodin XI.

CHAPTER
9

Lodin XI had about as much in common with Northpoint as a laser cannon had with a slingshot. The first hint of its complexity was the orbiting fuel stations; no world of Tradertowns out on the frontier had the money, or the volume of business, to erect such complex structures, which was why the *Deathmaker*, like almost all the ships of the frontier, was built for landing on planets.

But the fuel depots were only the first inkling of the sophistication of the planet. It was divided into seventeen different nations—also unheard of on the Tradertown worlds—each of which possessed from ten to fifty cities. At last count the native humanoid population spoke in eleven different languages and perhaps twice that many dialects. Democracy, republic, monarchy, and dictatorship all existed side by side with no visible discord. The race of Man had set up business and housekeeping quarters too, and now totaled almost four percent of Lodin XI's population.

The native structures were . . . alien. There seemed to be no logical progression to them. Where a street might be expected to widen, it vanished. Some one-floor structures were entirely transparent, while a number of the skyscrapers possessed no windows at all. Business districts were nonexistent. Huge stores and factories sprouted up in the midst of wildly discordant residential neighborhoods, which in turn were infringing on the spaceport and the open-air zoos. In the midst of all this architectural hodgepodge was an occasional acre or two that nobody had bothered to build on at all. Boulevards wound in and out of totally dissimilar areas with no apparent rhyme or reason, while some of the more important government agencies possessed no means of access other than unpaved desert.

Lane set the *Deathmaker* down in Freeport, a human colony on the outer edges of Belarba, the planet's largest center of commerce. He spent the remainder of the day making connections for his animals, deciding that the cost of shipping entire preserved carcasses would come to less than the price that native skinners and taxidermists would charge. He estimated that he'd be stuck on Lodin XI for at least a week before all his vouchers arrived, and he set out to find a suitable dwelling for the duration of his enforced stay.

Freeport was a large settlement, housing almost 150,000 humans, and as a result it was too specialized to offer a catch-all business of the type Tchaka ran. Lane picked the largest, most impressive-looking hotel he could find, was told that the Mufti would not be allowed inside his room, and settled for a somewhat lesser hotel with somewhat lesser restrictions.

Restrictions seemed to be the order of the day. No Lodinites were allowed inside Freeport without incredibly complex identification papers, and the Lodinites responded in kind, both toward the humans and—to a slighter degree—toward the numerous other colonies of sentient off-worlders that had grown up around Freeport.

There was a middle ground, an oddly-shaped sector which seemed to have a completely international—or interplanetary—aspect to it. It was kind of a no-man's-land between Freeport and Belarba, composed largely of cultural centers, restaurants and black-market dealerships. It was rumored that one could buy a slave of almost any race in the galaxy there; no one took the rumor seriously, which is doubtless why both the rumor and the practice persisted.

Lane had a lot of time on his hands, so he decided to visit such sights as the no-man's-land area offered him. First, as always, he sought out the museum.

Here, in brilliant imitations of life, were hundreds upon hundreds of strange, exotic creatures, almost all of them killed by men like himself to assuage the curiosity of those who didn't care or dare to follow him as he went out past the limits of the frontier.

The first thing that caught his eye was a Devilowl. Huge, horned, red-eyed, teeth jutting in all directions, truly Satanic in appearance, it had been masterfully stuffed and sewn together, but the taxidermist had obviously never seen Devilowls in action. The head was cocked at the wrong angle, and its legs were completely extended, which almost never occurred in nature.

He walked on to the aquatic exhibition, and stopped in front of a pair of Baffledivers. They had the familiar screenlike snouts that siphoned the water past their enormous bodies like jet engines, and the huge, razorlike fins and tail that could propel them so swiftly through the sea and slice their prey to ribbons. As he looked at the exhibit he wondered at the sanity of any man who would hunt them at the bottom of a sea where neither visibility nor maneuverability existed.

Then he saw the little plaque, written in eight of the major languages of Lodin XI, as well as Terran and Canphorite:

BAFFLEDIVERS

CARNIVORA NATIVE TO THE OCEANS OF
PINNIPES II, USUALLY FOUND AT A DEPTH
OF ONE KILOMETER OR MORE. THIS PAIR
SLAIN BY NICOBAR LANE, RACE OF MAN,
4062 G.E.

He shook his head in amazement, wondering how the hell he had ever survived the encounter.

He entered the Hall of Sentient Beings, where numerous signs told him repeatedly that none of these exhibits had been killed by hunters, but that all had been freely donated to the museum by the home worlds of the deceased. The display case for Man was empty, and the one for inhabitants of Lodin XI showed a little scene in which all the characters were clothed. All other sentient displays—and there were upward of fifty of them—contained unclad and awkwardly posed figures.

He continued walking, and every now and then came across more empty cases. Occasionally repair work was going on, but usually the cases had brasslike plates stating what would soon be on display.

At last he came to an enormous empty case, almost sixty yards across and half as high, and looked at the plaque:

RESERVED

FOR THE DREAMWISH BEAST

He wondered if anyone at the museum had the slightest idea of the creature's proportions or makeup. He became convinced that it was just a publicity gimmick when he came across four more empty cases, all much smaller, each reserved for the Deathdealer or some other of the creature's plethora of names.

"Lots of luck," he muttered to himself. Then, tiring of the museum, he walked out into the hot dry air and went to the art gallery, which was about two hundred yards away down a crazily winding street which broadened and narrowed even more insanely than it curved.

Taxidermy didn't differ much from world to world, but conceptions of art were as different as things ever got to be. The Lodinites used no paint or paint analogs. Almost all of their works were bas-relief sculptures, not quite abstract, but bearing no relationship to anything Lane had ever experienced. The colors were rather dull and tedious, but that was to be expected from a race whose perception of the color spectrum ranged only from yellow to blue. Lane lingered for a few minutes, trying to understand what he was looking at, but finally gave it up as a lost cause and went to the section of the building that housed human art.

There were the usual landscapes, seascapes, spacescapes, plump nudes, still lifes and imitation-Michelangelo sculptures. (Renaissance art was coming back into style again in the Deluros system, which meant that most other human worlds would be copying it just in time to be outmoded.)

Soon Lane grew restless. He had no more true interest in paint and canvas than he had in animals once they had been stuffed and mounted. He'd spent five hours trying to let a little culture seep in and was finally ready to admit that he was bored with it.

He spent the rest of the afternoon and the next two days in the library, trying without success to find some more information on the Starduster. He then spent another day browsing in

Freeport's two book/tape shops—one new, one antiquarian—with no success.

When he returned to his hotel from the second store he found a radio message waiting for him, to the effect that William Campbell Blessbull XXIII was terribly displeased with the condition of the shipment he had received from Lane. Four of the eleven animals were in stages of partial decomposition, and until they were replaced, no payment would be made on any portion of the order.

Lane had the message confirmed, then sent a message of his own, instructing his lawyer to sue Blessbull for the money due him on the seven acceptable specimens and to check out the condition of the other four.

Then, bored and fidgety, he went back to no-man's-land, looking for a little illicit excitement. Nothing there appealed to him, so he stopped by a black market dealer's shop and picked up forged papers giving him entry into Belarba.

The sun had just set when he walked into Belarba proper. He wasn't quite sure what he had expected—perhaps something like some of the more exotic native quarters he had been to on the frontier worlds—but Belarba was just another city. Different, to be sure, but not what he craved.

For one thing, he was intensely conscious of numerous unsubtle and unfriendly stares as he walked down the patternless streets. He stopped to eat in a native restaurant, but couldn't read the menu and, through a painfully embarrassing attempt at sign language, finally informed the waiter to order for him. He became very uncomfortable waiting in a chair that had been fashioned for beings that stored all their fat in their buttocks and had arms jointed almost at the shoulder. The arms of his chair seemed to enclose him like a cage, his back ached, and his legs were numb. He took only one brief look at the food that was finally slapped on his table by a surly busboy, paid his bill, and left without having eaten a mouthful.

A Lodinite bar was next on his agenda. The liquor was drinkable but packed no kick, and when a couple of natives began edging toward him he decided that discretion was the only reasonable part of valor.

After that he just wandered through the streets, trying to fathom the mentality that had created such patternless buildings and thoroughfares. It was like a bad dream. The Lodinites were just enough like Man so the structures and artifacts of their civilization bore a superficial resemblance to what he was used to. But upon closer scrutiny none of it made any sense. There were buildings without any means of ingress, stores that seemed to be giving their goods away to any passersby who looked mildly interested, factories constructing small wooden and metallic devices that seemed to be totally without function.

Finally his mind could assimilate no more, and he decided to return to no-man's-land. It was then that he discovered, much to his disgust, that the hunter who had footslogged through a thousand jungles was completely lost.

He spent the next two hours following twisting streets that doubled back into themselves or came to abrupt stops against buildings or in empty fields. Finally he saw another member of his race walking on the opposite side of the throughfare and rather shamefacedly admitted his problem.

"Just ask one of the Lodinites," said the man.

"I can't," said Lane. "I don't know their language."

"Then how did you get your papers cleared, unless . . . ?" His expression hardened. "Being in Belarba illegally is a felony. You know that, don't you?"

"Mister, as far as I'm concerned, just being a Belarban is a felony. All I want to know is how to get the hell out of this madhouse."

The instructions were very complex, for Lane had wandered quite a distance from no-man's-land. It took him until an hour after sunrise to find his way back to his hotel.

He slept for the remainder of the day, bothered only by the now-familiar nightmares, then arose in the cool of the evening. He shaved, showered, dressed, and tried to decide where to go. He still hadn't sampled any of Freeport's whorehouses or drug dens, and he'd heard talk of a freak show presenting endless perversions, but he couldn't work up any great enthusiasm for any of them. He ordered a bottle of Cygnian cognac from room service and sat on his bed, staring out the window with dark, brooding eyes.

He looked out past the boundaries of the city, into the vast red-brown desert beyond. Then his gaze rose, until he was looking into the clear night sky.

It was up there somewhere, feeding off the dust cloud, glowing a dull reddish-orange, floating effortlessly through the void. In its own way it was a thing of beauty, flawed here and there as only true beauty can be.

It was also a thing of immense power. Not the power to move mountains or build cities or destroy planets—that power was reserved for Man. But it had power nonetheless, the power to assimilate a million little deaths and hurl them back into the face of its attacker, the power to return every hint of doom to its doombringer. No, no sane man, having experienced that once, would ever willingly subject himself to it again.

And, with an honesty that was almost too painful to bear, he finally acknowledged what he had known for months.

He enjoyed it.

CHAPTER
10

Lane walked across the campus, trying not to feel too much like a living antique. He stopped a couple of students, asked directions, and finally came to the office building he sought.

He took an escalating ramp to the sixth level, got off, and walked down a long, shiny, well-lighted corridor, counting the doors as he did so. When he came to the office he wanted, he knocked once and entered.

The room, though overloaded with books, tapes, papers, and various alien artifacts, was nonetheless even neater than the outer corridor. Frilly little white things hung down over the windows, and a vase filled with freshly cut flowers took up the right-hand corner of the large desk that sat in the middle of the room. And sitting at the desk was a caricature so blatant that no cartoonist would have dared to imitate it.

She was a little old lady. Wrong, corrected Lane: she was *the* Little Old Lady, replete with short, fluffy gray hair, cherubic cheeks, about forty excess pounds on her small frame, and a smile that most doting grandmothers would have given their remaining teeth for.

"Yes?" she said, looking up. "What can I do for you, young man?"

Lane smiled. "It's been a long time since I was a young man, but thank you anyway. I'm looking for Ondine Gillian."

"And now you've found her," said the woman, returning his smile.

"You?" said Lane. "Somehow you're not quite what I pictured."

"The name," said Ondine, nodding cheerfully. "Most people expect some will-o'-the-wisp sea-nymph who wears mollusk shells in her hair."

"Not at all," said Lane. "I expected an austere, rather severe woman who would throw my message into the trash can."

"Message?" she said. "Then you must be Mr. Lane."

"Correct," said Lane. "And may I say that you bear no resemblance to the cold-blooded, analytical, emotionless woman who wrote the monographs I've read."

"Why, thank you so much," she said, her eyes twinkling. "Won't you pull up a chair and sit down, Mr. Lane?"

Lane shut the door behind him and pulled a chair over to the desk. As he did so, Ondine handed him a three-dimensional photograph.

"Six of my grandchildren," she said with a note of pride. "My son, who occasionally forgets that our family did not begin with his birth, finally got around to sending it to me this morning."

Lane looked at the children, none of whom appeared half so cherubic as their grandmother, and made appropriate polite noises.

"Can I offer you a cup of tea?" asked Ondine.

"Tea?" repeated Lane. "I haven't had tea in, oh, it must be twenty years. Yes, I'd appreciate that."

Even before he had finished the sentence, Ondine had scurried over to the wall, slid back a panel, grabbed a metal teapot, and poured the contents into a small china cup.

"Sugar?" she asked, hovering over him as he tentatively took a sip.

"To tell the truth, I don't remember," said Lane.

"I'd advise against it. It's bad for the teeth."

"I'll take your word for it," said Lane, taking another sip. "It's very good."

"It's even better with lemon," said Ondine. "Can I get you some?"

"No, thanks," said Lane. "Please sit down."

"I'm sorry," said Ondine, who didn't look sorry at all. "Sometimes I get a little overenthused, especially with the children all grown and gone. I know its considered terribly gauche, but I do so love *doing* for people."

"Which brings me to the subject of my visit," said Lane. "I need some help, though not of a maternal nature."

"I'd be delighted, Mr. Lane," said Ondine. "It's so rare that anyone, except for an occasional student, comes up here to see me. I've certainly no wish to chase you away, but may I ask why you have sought me out?"

"Of course," said Lane. "From what I've been able to ascertain, you are the leading living authority on ancient nonhuman civilizations in the vicinity of the dust cloud. I happen to be extremely interested in that area."

"Oh, bosh!" she said, blushing slightly. "I've done a little research on some of the planetary cultures in that area, but certainly I'm not the leading authority even within the confines of this university. I'm just an old woman who decided not to wither away waiting for her children to remember to come to dinner every now and then."

"You're too modest," said Lane.

"You're too kind," Ondine replied, smiling. "By the way, have you seen it?"

"Ma'am?" said Lane, puzzled.

"Why, the Dreamwish Beast, of course. Have you seen it already, or are you just setting out to find it? That *is* why you're here, is it not?'' She smiled sweetly and poured him another cup of tea.

"I've seen it,'' said Lane, who decided that Ondine Gillian wasn't quite as pink and fluffy as she looked.

"I thought so,'' she said cheerfully.

"I want to know everything you can tell me about it,'' said Lane. "Fact, fable, myth, legend, tall tales, I don't care. I'll sort them all out later.''

"What exactly is your interest in it, Mr. Lane?''

"I'm a hunter.''

"And you wish to kill the Dreamwish Beast?''

"I'm not sure,'' said Lane. "For the moment, I just want to learn a little more about it.''

"Has some museum financed you?'' asked Ondine.

He shook his head. "I'm independent. Besides, no museum will be able to use the thing. At least, not until they find a way to stuff and mount a ball of energy.''

"Where did you see it?'' asked Ondine.

"The first time was near Pinnipes. It ducked around a black hole and I lost it.''

"The first time?'' Suddenly she frowned. It was replaced an instant later by the smile which Lane suspected was the protective coloring of a woman who was far more intellectually formidable than she wanted anyone to know. "Have you seen it since?''

"Twice,'' said Lane.

"That's very interesting,'' said Ondine. "May I offer you a muffin to go with your tea?''

Lane shook his head.

"Very well,'' she said, looking disappointed, but taking one herself. "Where shall I begin? At the beginning, I suppose. The Dreamwish Beast has cropped up, in one form or another, in nine different cultures of the dustcloud area. In each case, the races in question had developed interstellar travel, which would certainly lead me to believe that it doesn't ever get too close to a planetary system. May I get you a cushion to sit on?"

"No, thank you," said Lane. "Please continue."

"Certainly," said Ondine, flashing him another smile. "The oldest reference to it comes from the Lemm, an amphibious race that had space travel when Man was still swinging in trees and looking for grubworms—although it is my own belief that *Australopithicus africanus* had no more tree-climbing ability than I do. The feet simply weren't made for it. All that talk about tree-climbing is just a lot of rubbish, don't you agree?"

"I have no opinion," said Lane, grinning. "You seem to end every paragraph with a question."

"I'm sorry, Mr. Lane," said Ondine. "It's a nervous little habit of mine. I suppose it's to force people to listen to what I'm saying. You have no idea how effective it can be when I'm lecturing to a classful of rather bored students. Of course, my own children continually disregard it, but I suppose one can't have everything."

"Getting back to the Lemm . . ." said Lane tentatively.

"Ah, yes, the Lemm. Being amphibious, as I said, they were interested only in water worlds, and ultimately they came to Pinnipes II. Evidently they found conditions there to be too harsh"—Lane chuckled at that—"but somewhere on the journey there or back they came across a life form in interstellar space. Since we have yet to find any other creature that can live in the void, and since later legends and sightings, including your own, have placed it within a reasonable distance of the Pinnipes system, I believe that this creature was indeed the Dreamwish Beast."

"Did they leave behind any description of it?" asked Lane.

"I'm afraid not, Mr. Lane," said Ondine. "You must remember that they had only a passing interest in it, or in anything else that didn't pertain to water worlds. I stumbled over a reference to it during my readings and deduced the rest.''

"How long ago was this?"

"My research, or the sighting?" asked Ondine.

"The sighting," said Lane.

"At least a million years; probably closer to a million and a half.''

"Too long," said Lane.

"I beg your pardon?" said Ondine.

"I'd like to find out how long it takes to make one complete circuit of its feeding grounds," said Lane. "That would give me an idea where to find it at any given time. However, that's too far back. It must have gone back and forth a number of times since then. Please continue.''

"The next legitimate reference to it comes from the race of Dorne, from the planetary system of Belore," said Ondine.

"Didn't we kill off the Dornes in a war a couple of thousand years ago?" asked Lane.

"Almost," said Ondine. "A handful survived, and the remnants of the race exist even today, though I believe there are only one hundred or so left.''

"What did they have to say about the creature?" asked Lane.

"Quite a lot," replied Ondine. "In fact, they seem to have built their entire culture upon the Dreamwish Beast.''

"Why would anyone do that?" said Lane, genuinely puzzled.

"I rather hoped *you* might have some suggestion along that line," said Ondine. "It appears that the Dornes and the Dreamwish Beasts were blood enemies—at least according to the Dornes.''

"Dreamwish *Beasts*?" said Lane. "There was more than one?"

"Of course," said Ondine. "There seems to have been an

entire race of them. The Dornes' history is unclear, which is not unexpected after all this time, but it appears that at one point the Dornes went hunting for the beasts, probably as a ritualistic rite of passage into adulthood. According to everything I can find on the subject, they were quite convinced they had killed off all of the beasts. When I first came across the references to the Dreamwish Beast among the other cultures, I assumed that they were simply myths based on the legends of the Dornes. But there have been too many sightings by members of our own race, who couldn't possibly have had any contact with the Dorne culture, for me to doubt that at least one Dreamwish Beast escaped the slaughter.''

''What weapons did they use?'' asked Lane.

''The Dornes? I have absolutely no idea. My interests have never run along those lines, Mr. Lane. Anyway, sometime either during or immediately after the killing, a drastic change overcame the Dorne culture. They became a race of death-worshipers. Not life after death, like the ancient Egyptians, but death as an end in itself. I believe that they're the only such culture in the known galaxy.''

''Dreamwish Beast seems to be its most common name,'' said Lane. ''How did it come about?''

''I'm not really sure,'' said Ondine. ''There's an old legend about a shipful of human explorers who ran into it centuries ago. Theoretically the creature somehow impressed such horrible dreams and nightmares upon them that they either went mad or died. It's completely unauthenticated, to be sure, and I don't believe it for a minute''—she paused for a breath and shot a quick glance at him—''but a few centuries of retelling could result not only in a name like Dreamwish Beast, but in Deathdealer as well. As for Sunlighter and the other names, I have no knowledge whatsoever of their origins. You must remember, Mr. Lane, that this creature is peripheral to my main interest; I have never attempted to make a study of it, and know of it only in relation to the cultures that I *am* studying.''

''You can add another name to the list,'' said Lane. ''Starduster.''

''Starduster,'' she repeated. ''Yes, that would certainly fit, wouldn't it? And of course it's very colorful. I fully approve of it, Mr. Lane. Is it your own creation?''

''No,'' said Lane. ''I don't call it anything. It was coined by an old man that the creature killed. I don't even know what his name was.''

''What a shame,'' said Ondine earnestly. ''Were you there, Mr. Lane?''

He nodded.

''Why weren't you killed too, if I may ask?''

''He was a used-up old man,'' said Lane.

''You might have said that you were a vigorous young man,'' said Ondine. ''But let it pass.''

''I meant no disrespect,'' said Lane.

''I know,'' said Ondine, putting her smile back on. ''I'm just a little sensitive to such things these days. Can you tell me how your companion was killed?''

''It seems to have a defensive mechanism the likes of which I've never run across before,'' said Lane. He described it in detail, including the death of the Mariner and his most recent meeting with the creature, only omitting his own reaction to it.

''Fascinating!'' said Ondine. ''And of course, it explains an enormous amount about the explorers who went mad. However,'' she added, her brow furrowed, ''it doesn't quite explain the Dorne culture, does it?''

''I suppose not,'' said Lane.

''Is there anything *you* can tell *me* about the Dreamwish Beast?''

''Well, the creature is about seven miles in diameter,

roughly spherical in shape, no visible sensory or locomotive organs of any type, kind of a dull red-orange in color, it gives off a sizable infrared reading, and it's fully capable of attaining light speeds."

"And, of course, the Bible would approve of it," said Ondine.

"I'm afraid I don't quite follow you," said Lane.

"Whatever harm you do to it comes right back at you," said Ondine. "I can't imagine any better example of the old saying about an eye for an eye."

"Perhaps," said Lane.

Ondine glanced at her old-fashioned wristwatch. "Oh, my goodness!" she exclaimed. "I hadn't even noticed the time. I'm afraid I'm going to have to run, Mr. Lane. It's my eldest granddaughter's birthday tomorrow, and I've hardly bought her any presents at all."

"How many grandchildren do you have?" asked Lane.

"Eleven," she said proudly.

"Buying presents for all of them must be quite a strain."

"What's a grandmother for?" she said with a chuckle. "Besides, if it wasn't for me, their birthdays and the holidays would slip by completely unnoticed by their parents." She wrinkled her stubby little nose at the thought. Then she pulled out a piece of paper, began writing on it, and finally handed it over to Lane.

"You'll be wanting to speak to a Dorne, of course," she said. "They don't have much use for Men, but this should serve as an introduction to one of them who has proved quite useful to my studies. His name is Vostuvian."

"Thank you," said Lane. He looked at the paper and was unable to read a word of it.

Ondine was scurrying around the office, washing out the teacup and cleaning a few crumbs away from in front of the muffin container, as Lane walked to the door.

"Oh, Mr. Lane," she called after him.

"Yes?" he said, turning to her.

"The dust cloud is trillions upon trillions of cubic miles in volume, isn't it?"

Lane nodded.

"The odds against any two things, even stars, meeting within the cloud are literally astronomical, aren't they?"

"Yes."

"Then if I were you," she said, picking up a rag and beginning to clean off her desk, "I think I would ask myself why I had met the Dreamwish Beast three times already."

CHAPTER

II

Belore was a dirty world, dirty and dry and dusty. Here and there one could find a little water, barely enough for the sustenance of life. Once there had been more, once there had been shining cities alive with trade and commerce, and people had flowed through the streets and across the fertile plains, proud and happy and hopeful. Now the cities were decaying ruins, the commerce and trade a distant memory, and the people a downtrodden remnant of what had once been a strong and vigorous race.

Lane made his way across a dusty field to a little row of mud-caked shanties, forty-one in number, housing what was left of the Dornes. Elsewhere on the planet was a gleaming Tradertown, and a number of refining and smelting plants, but the Dornes had no interest or intercourse with any of the alien races that had set up shop on their world. They sat, and ate, and slept, and waited for the last member of their race to die.

As Lane reached the nearest of the shanties, he got his first look at a Dorne. It was a male, strikingly humanoid in appearance, standing about seven feet tall, unbelievably gaunt, bald, with enormous bulging eyes and broad, wide-set nostrils. Each hand possessed three fingers and a pair of opposing thumbs, and the arms and legs were jointed very close to the hands and feet, but the overall effect was not too discordant.

Lane walked up to the Dorne.

"Can you tell me where I can find Vostuvian?" he asked.

The Dorne simply stared at him.

Lane tried once more in Terran, then repeated the question in Galactic, Camphorian, two Terrazane dialects, and even the bastard humanoid tongue that had cropped up on the frontiers. The Dorne's expression never changed.

"Vostuvian," repeated Lane, growing impatient.

No answer.

He had just about made up his mind to go from shanty to shanty until he found a Dorne who answered to the name when he heard a low voice, almost a whisper, from behind him.

"I am Vostuvian."

He turned and found himself facing another Dorne. At first they appeared to be identical, but upon closer scrutiny he was able to spot minute differences in facial and skeletal structure between them. And, of course, the rags each wore were of different colors and lengths.

"You speak Terran?"

"When I must," said Vostuvian. "I much prefer not to, but I do not suppose that you can speak Beloran."

"Not yet," said Lane.

Vostuvian made a slight motion, a swaying of his hips while the rest of his body remained rigid, and immediately the other Dorne walked off, leaving him alone with Lane.

"Who are you?" said Vostuvian in the half-whisper which Lane assumed was the normal Dorne speaking voice. It puzzled him, as the Dornes' ears were mere holes in the sides of their heads, and very small holes at that. "Why do you know my name, and what business have you with the race of Dorne?"

Lane pulled out Ondine's note and handed it to the Dorne, who glanced at it briefly and let it drop to the ground, where a hot breeze blew it away.

"What is your interest in the *straigor*?"

"What is a *straigor*?" asked Lane. "Is that your term for the Dreamwish Beast?"

"No," said Vostuvian. "Dreamwish Beast is *your* term for the *straigor*. However, as a courtesy to you, I shall use your name for it. You still have not answered my question."

"I'm a hunter," said Lane. "I want to learn more about this creature."

"You are too late," said Vostuvian. "The last Dreamwish Beast was killed by my race many eons ago."

"Not so," said Lane. "I saw one not six Standard months ago."

"Impossible," said Vostuvian. "Describe it."

Lane did so in minute detail. When he finished he watched Vostuvian for some change in expression, however slight. There was none.

"It was a Dreamwish Beast," said the Dorne. He sat down on the dirt, and Lane did likewise. "The question now presents itself: Which of the two—you, by action, or the Dreamwish Beast, by inaction—do I find it less repugnant to help?" He closed his eyes and sat motionless, not even breathing, for the better part of three minutes. Finally he turned to Lane.

"What do you wish to know?"

"How can I kill a Dreamwish Beast without dying myself?"

"The same problem once confronted my race," said Vostuvian. "Originally we were completely unable to slay the Dreamwish Beasts by any means whatever. Then, as we studied them more thoroughly, we devised a weapon that killed them, but we were unable to survive it ourselves. Finally, we perfected the weapon to the point where it destroyed them so swiftly that they were unable to transmit their pain back to us.''

"How did this weapon work?" asked Lane.

"When perfected," said the Dorne, "it was the first—and possibly the only—practical application of the entropy principle."

"Would you clarify that?"

"The Dreamwish Beast is a life form composed of energy. Our weapon diluted that energy, draining it away by dissipating it. Ultimately, by the siphoning off of their energy, the creatures were degraded to the lowest energy level of the universe."

"Just like that?" said Lane with a smile.

"Just like that," said Vostuvian, still expressionless.

"I don't suppose you have any of those entropy weapons lying around?"

Vostuvian pointed toward the pathetic little row of huts. "What do you think?"

"Do any Dornes still know the principles that went into the weapon?" asked Lane.

"Yes," said Vostuvian.

"You?"

"Yes," said Vostuvian.

"Why haven't you built one?"

"To what purpose?" said Vostuvian. "In another century my race will be extinct whether I build one or not."

Lane scratched his head and tried to understand the mentality of a race that had the key to the weapon that had just been described to him, a weapon that might conceivably drive all the many alien invaders off the face of Belore forever, and instead of building it chose to live out its collective life in filth and squalor. Suddenly Vostuvian seemed a little more alien to him.

"If I supply the materials, could you build such a weapon for me?"

"Yes," said Vostuvian.

"What will you need?" asked Lane.

Vostuvian rattled off a list of the necessary components.

"Too expensive," said Lane. "And it would take too long to round up all the parts. Maybe I'd better stick to the vibrator."

"What is a vibrator?" asked Vostuvian.

Lane explained the principles of the weapon to him. "Even in space it has an effective range of almost twenty thousand miles, possibly a little more, and it hits with the impact of an enormous sledgehammer."

"You cannot kill the Dreamwish Beast with your vibrator," said Vostuvian tonelessly.

"I've killed little pieces of it already," said Lane.

"You have not," said Vostuvian.

"Yes I have," said Lane. "I felt it."

"What makes you think that you and the Dreamwish Beast have the same sensory perceptions?" said the Dorne.

"What are you talking about?" said Lane, suddenly apprehensive.

"What feels hot to you may feel cold, or wet, or like nothing at all, to a creature as different in nature as the Dreamwish Beast. Your hunger may be its drowsiness, your agony its mild exuberance."

"An interesting hypothesis, nothing more," said Lane. "I know what I felt."

"It is not a hypothesis," said Vostuvian. "It is fact. You do not know even yet what you felt." He paused for a moment, then continued. "The Dreamwish Beasts are no more dense than the dust cloud that gives them sustenance. They rarely approach any planetary bodies. They can do us no physical harm. Why do you think my race decided to wage a war of extermination against them?"

"I have no idea," said Lane.

"Because, killer of animals, physical harm is the least of

the things a sentient being can suffer; we react far more to mental and emotional stimuli. The Dornes' initial weapons were not unlike your vibrator, and the creatures' reactions were similar, if not identical, to the reaction of the beast you encountered. We, too, thought we were experiencing the preliminary death throes of the creatures."

Vostuvian closed his eyes again, remaining rigid and motionless except for the twitching of one of his toes. Then, as if nothing had happened, he relaxed, opened his eyes, and continued speaking.

"We became addicted to what we considered to be a premonition of death. It shocked our systems, but nonetheless produced a craving for more such encounters. Our entire culture began to evolve and change into something that worshiped death and disdained life, for nothing in our racial experience had affected us so deeply as the inkling of death the beasts emitted. Then, many millennia later, we invented the first crude weapons based on the entropy principle. These really did kill the creatures, and ourselves as well. There was no similarity between what we had felt before and what we felt now. It was then that we realized our original weapons hadn't harmed the creatures at all."

"What *had* they done?" said Lane, an empty feeling in the pit of his stomach.

"Pleased them," said Vostuvian. "Pleased them beyond all measure; and, subsequently, pleased us beyond all measure as well. In retrospect, we should have realized that. There is no joy or pleasure in death, which is the termination of everything; but we had never experienced another race's emotions, and we had misread ecstasy for anguish, sensuality for morbidity. Do you understand what I am saying to you?"

"Yes," said Lane. And in that instant, he knew the answer to Ondine Gillian's question about why he had found the Dreamwish Beast three times. *It* had found *him*.

He stared at the ground for a long time, trying to collect

his thoughts and analyze his emotions. To admit that he had gotten some perverse kind of thrill from death had been difficult enough, even though he made his living from killing things. But *this* was something else again, something he wasn't ready to come to grips with.

And suddenly he was overwhelmed with anger and outrage. As his fury flowed over him, washing away his other emotions before he could sort them out, he felt a sudden kinship with Vostuvian. Now he knew why the Dreamwish Beasts had become the Dornes' blood enemy, and he knew that the one remaining creature had just become his mortal enemy as well.

"It will take about two years," he said aloud.

"You will send me the material for the entropy weapon," said Vostuvian. It was a statement, not a question.

"Yes. What will you charge me to construct it?"

"Nothing. The death of the Dreamwish Beast will be payment enough. I will come with you."

"Not a chance," said Lane.

"How will you find it?" said Vostuvian.

"I won't have to," said Lane, suppressing a shudder. "It will find me."

"Not if you have the weapon," said the Dorne. "It knows."

Lane stared long and hard at Vostuvian. "Why should I believe you?" he said at last.

"If you can think of a single reason why I should lie to you, then you should not believe me," said Vostuvian.

"You may want to kill it yourself," said Lane.

"If so, why would I have told you about the entropy weapon?" countered the Dorne.

"As an inducement to get me to take you along," said Lane.

"You are not thinking clearly," said Vostuvian.

"Maybe not," said Lane. "But you're not coming along, and that's final."

"You will not be able to kill the Dreamwish Beast without me."

"I'll find it, all right," said Lane grimly.

"I didn't say that you would not find it," said Vostuvian. "I said that you would not be able to kill it."

"Just have that weapon ready when I need it," said Lane. He got to his feet, dusted himself off, and began walking away.

"Two years, three years, a dozen," Vostuvian whispered after Lane's retreating figure. "Sooner or later you will need me, and I shall be here, waiting."

His words seemed to hang suspended in time and space as Lane walked to the *Deathmaker*.

CHAPTER
12

The *Deathmaker* raced silently through the void, two years out of port.

Three times in the past twenty Standard months it had set down: once to purchase most of the components for the entropy weapon, once to ship those components to Belore, and once to close out a number of bank accounts while fueling up. Now the ship was headed back to Northpoint, where the remainder of Lane's money was tied up.

It had been a long trip. Twice Lane thought he had come across the Dreamwish Beast, but both times he was mistaken. Even the Mufti was bored, so much so that Lane had already given it a pair of hundred-day Deepsleeps. He wished that there were a less tedious way of getting his hands on his remaining funds, but the economic capitals of the Democracy didn't have much financial truck with the frontier worlds, especially those that refused to deal in credits, and there was nothing to do but pick up the money in person. So he spent hours each day going through his rigorous anti-boredom routines and rituals, and tried to ignore the nightmares that had long since spilled over into his waking hours.

Elsewhere, important things were happening. The Democracy was starting to crumble around the edges. The credit had to be backed with uranium, then platinum, and finally on faith alone; and it was becoming obvious that there was not an abundance of faith to be found. A strike of the Federated Miners had brought the human-controlled section of the galaxy almost to a standstill for more than a month before the beleaguered government yielded to their demands. A cure had finally been discovered for eplasia, a blood disease that had cropped up three centuries back and become quite widespread. Two hundred seventy-eight more life forms, including Sillyworms, had become extinct, and one hundred sixteen new ones had been discovered on the frontier.

Of all this Lane was ignorant, nor would he have cared about it had he known. Lane had no more interest in governments than they had in him. None of his money was tied up in credits. Diseases became important to him only after he contracted them. The miners didn't affect him directly. As for the extinct animals—well, as long as new species kept replacing the old ones, he wouldn't be hurting for work.

In fact, he wasn't hurting for work right now. The Vainmill Syndicate had twice gone to the vast expense of contacting him in space and requesting certain species for their museums. He had replied affirmatively to both requests, but as yet hadn't gone to work on either of them.

His sole concern now, as it had been for more than two years, was the destruction of the Dreamwish Beast. First he had to get the weapon assembled—he had already dubbed it the diluter—and then he had to use it on his intended victim. Then he would pick up the pieces of his career, scrap the weapon for what money he could get back out of it, and once again submerge his emotions as he went about his task of sophisticated bloodletting.

Lane glanced at his control panel for perhaps the millionth time. Twenty-seven more days to Northpoint. It was time to put in to port, to go on a binge, sleep on a real bed instead of a hammock, eat a real meal and wash it down with a liter or two of Tchaka's best beer. A little rest, a little fresh air, maybe a day or two with a woman, and he'd be ready to prepare for the final phase of the hunt.

And then he saw it.

He didn't know where it came from, or what it was doing this far from the dust cloud, if it was tracking him or taunting him. But it was there, seventy thousand miles off his starboard bow, almost sixty degrees of arc below the ship.

He cursed under his breath and decided to keep the *Deathmaker* on its course. The creature closed to within fifty thousand miles.

He checked his sensing devices to make sure that his main control panel hadn't picked up a ship. It was indeed the creature. He debated for a moment, then increased the *Deathmaker*'s speed to maximum. The creature kept pace with him.

They remained thus for six hours. Then slowly, inexorably, the creature began narrowing the gap between them, and Lane began evasive maneuvering. It didn't work.

When the creature got within twenty thousand miles, he began to feel the tension spread throughout him, and was unable to tell whether it was his own emotion or the creature's. But whichever of them it originated with, it was getting stronger by the second, and was tinged with a little thrill of anticipation.

He shook his head vigorously and began singing at the top of his lungs, trying to drown out the sensation, and failing.

Now the creature was within fifteen thousand miles, now twelve, and he knew that he would never reach Northpoint without coming to grips with it. His entire body was sweating and trembling, and he forgot first the words and then the melody to his song.

Though he knew it would do no good, he trained the laser cannon on the creature and fired it. Then, with the same sense of futility, he fired the molecular imploder.

"Go away!" he screamed at the main viewscreen, where

the creature had just become visible. "I'm not ready for you yet!"

But the creature did not go away. It closed to six thousand miles, throbbing and pulsating. Lane slowed the *Deathmaker* to a crawl, hoping that the creature would overshoot it so much that he might buy a little maneuvering time, but the creature did no such thing. It stopped almost as swiftly as the ship, and now was less than five hundred miles away.

Lane's feelings were no different than on his prior meetings with it, but now that he could interpret them he felt horribly unclean. He fired the laser cannon again, and again there was no reaction.

And then, with a hoarse sound that was halfway between a scream and a sob, he pressed the vibrator's firing mechanism.

The emotional jolt was as powerful as before, but this time it took him only a minute or two to regain his faculties. He checked his panel and saw that the creature was retreating rapidly, as it had done before.

He collapsed back into his chair, only then realizing that he had been standing for several minutes, and began shaking like a leaf. This time, he knew, the shaking was his own.

The creature was racing away, and would be beyond the range of his instrument panel in another two or three minutes. His mind and his emotions were his own again, and it would only take a few seconds to put the *Deathmaker* back on its course for Northpoint. The creature would keep until he was properly armed. The important thing now was to get to Northpoint and get his hands on the money he needed to complete the construction of the diluter.

But as he reached toward his navigational control panel, he knew that he wasn't going to Northpoint at all.

CHAPTER
13

Lane sat, silent and unmoving, in his office. His eyes were opened, but seemed to be focused on some very distant point that only he could discern. The Mufti clung to the ceiling, chattering quietly to itself. In the hangar that adjoined the office three mechanics were working on the *Deathmaker*.

There was a knock at the door. Lane didn't move, and the knock became more insistent. Finally the door opened to reveal Tchaka in all his metallic, multicolored glory.

"Nicobar!" he cried in a loud, booming voice.

Lane glanced at him but said nothing.

"It's been more than five years," said Tchaka. "When did you get in?"

"Last night," said Lane.

"And you didn't come to Tchaka's?"

"I wasn't thirsty."

"Then come over now," said Tchaka. "The first drink is always on the house."

"I don't drink anymore," said Lane.

"You must have lost your mind in space." Tchaka laughed. "It's high time you got your feet on the ground again."

He walked closer and peered at Lane through the semi-darkness. The hunter's hair, once a rich, thick, wavy brown, was now thin and white; his eyes were sunken and black-rimmed, his body thin and undernourished, his fingers long and clawlike, his cheeks bony and protruding.

"What the hell has happened to you, Nicobar?" said Tchaka. "If you walked into the bar I wouldn't recognize you."

"Five years is a long time," said Lane. "People change."

"Not like this," said Tchaka. "What happened?"

"Nothing."

"Then why did you liquidate all your assets?" said Tchaka. "Nothing like that happens in Hellhaven without Tchaka knowing about it. As soon as I heard it I knew you had to be back in town, and when I couldn't find you at my place I came over here. Why do you need all that money, Nicobar?"

"None of your business," said Lane.

"I can't agree with you, Nicobar." Tchaka smiled. "Anything that costs me a good customer is my business, and if you spend all this money somewhere else you can't spend it at Tchaka's."

"Somehow, I think Tchaka's will survive without my business," said Lane.

"True," said Tchaka. "But Tchaka's won't give up your business without a fight. What's happened to you?"

"Nothing," said Lane. "Why don't you just get the hell out of here?"

"Because I feel like talking," said Tchaka. He walked to the wall, took a screecher off Lane's weapon rack, and bent it out of shape with his right hand. "Shall we have a little chat now, Nicobar?"

"Not until you pay me for the screecher," said Lane.

"I'll give you twice its value in trade," said Tchaka. He looked around for a chair, discovered that Lane was sitting on the only one, and settled for leaning against a wall. "The last time I saw you you were studying a bunch of decaying old star maps. As I recall, it had something to do with the Dreamwish Beast. Ever find it?''

Lane nodded.

"Did you kill it?"

"No, I didn't."

"Must be some beast, if Nicobar Lane can't kill it."

"I'll kill it, all right," said Lane with the first show of emotion Tchaka had seen.

"Is that what you're doing here?" said Tchaka. "Getting money together to help you kill it?"

Lane nodded again. "It takes a special weapon. I've got to build it."

"First you've got to find the Dreamwish Beast again," said Tchaka. "It's a big galaxy."

"I'll find it," said Lane grimly.

"Just because you've seen it once or twice doesn't mean you can find it at will."

"Not once or twice," said Lane. "Nine times."

"Nine?" repeated Tchaka, staring at the haunted eyes that seemed to be looking right through him.

"Nine," said Lane. "Twice before I left here the last time, once more between here and Lodin . . ." His voice trailed off into nothingness for a moment. "And six more times since I left Belore."

"Belore?" said Tchaka. "What is there to hunt on Belore?"

"Nothing."

"Then what were you doing there?"

"Seeing a being that can assemble the weapon."

"Has he completed it?"

"I don't know," said Lane.

"This isn't like you, Nicobar," said Tchaka. "You kept alive all this time by attending to details, and now you tell me that you don't even know if your dream-killer has been built yet. How long has the Beloran had to work on it?"

"Four years, more or less," said Lane.

"Four years is a long time," said Tchaka. "It should be done by now."

"I suppose so."

"Then why haven't you got it?"

"I've been out of touch the past two years," said Lane.

"Where?" said Tchaka.

"In space."

"Doing what?"

"Don't ask," said Lane. "Just let it drop, Tchaka."

"So you've seen the Dreamwish Beast six times in the past two years." Tchaka smiled. "So what? Why do you chase it if you can't kill it?"

"Shut up," said Lane softly.

"Seems wasteful to me," said Tchaka. "Think of all the money you wasted on fuel and food. You'd have been a lot better off to have spent it here, Nicobar. No space-spawned monster can please you like one of Tchaka's girls."

"*Shut up!*" screamed Lane, jumping to his feet.

"Or can it?" said Tchaka, his face lighting up. "Is that it, Nicobar? Is that what you've been doing up there?"

Lane took a swing at Tchaka. The huge man caught his fist in mid-blow, smiled again, and squeezed until Lane fell to his knees with a cry of anguish.

"You should know better than that, Nicobar," he said with a laugh. "When Tchaka dies it will be from pleasure, not punishment. If I let you go are you going to try to attack me again?"

There was no response, and Tchaka squeezed harder.

"All right," whispered Lane between clenched teeth.

"Very reasonable," said Tchaka. "I hope you're as severe with your enemies as you are with your friends." He chuckled, then helped Lane to his feet. "Tell me about it, Nicobar."

"There's nothing to tell," said Lane, flexing his fingers painfully.

"We're not going through all that again, are we?" said Tchaka. "Tell me about the Dreamwish Beast."

"It's about seven miles in diameter," said Lane mechanically, "reddish-orange in color, no visible—"

"Tell me what it did to you, Nicobar," said Tchaka. "I don't give a damn what it looks like."

"It hasn't done anything to me," said Lane.

"You've aged thirty years, all the meat is off your bones, it evidently scared the life out of you—and you say it's done nothing? Let's try again, Nicobar."

"All right," said Lane slowly. "You remember when I told you about its defense mechanism?"

"That it throws pain and death back at you?" said Tchaka. "Yes, I remember."

"Well, I was wrong."

"I thought so," said Tchaka. "I never did believe in— what was it you called it?—a sending empath."

"The term still applies," said Lane.

"But you just said—"

"That it doesn't throw death back at me. I know what I said."

"You're not being very clear, Nicobar," said Tchaka.

"What I felt wasn't pain or death, Tchaka," said Lane, forcing each word out with an enormous effort. "Do you understand now?"

Tchaka's whole face lit up. His artificial eye began blinking and sparkling faster and brighter than Lane had ever seen it, and every one of his golden teeth was visible as he threw back his head and laughed.

"Why didn't you say so in the first place?" he boomed. "A new thrill, a new pleasure! And here I was, thinking my good friend had gone and become a necrophiliac! What's the problem, Nicobar? Why didn't you just sit back and enjoy it?''

"*Enjoy it?*" rasped Lane. "Enjoy that *thing*?"

"Of course!" thundered Tchaka. "I know men who have traversed half the galaxy looking for new sensations, who would sell their souls for just the briefest, tiniest taste of something different, and here you went out and discovered it by accident. That's what I call luck!"

"You haven't felt it," said Lane. "You haven't had those damned sensations inside your head."

"Evidently they can't be so terrible," said Tchaka, "or you wouldn't have spent the last two years chasing it all over space for six more doses."

"It's terrible, all right," whispered Lane, staring blindly at some point behind Tchaka's head. "You don't know."

"I know this," said Tchaka. "If it was me instead of you, I wouldn't be trying to kill the damned thing. I'd be trying to figure out what it's got and learn how to bottle it. This thing could be worth a fortune, Nicobar."

"It's got to die," said Lane softly.

"Why? Because it makes you feel perverted? Because it shames or disgusts you? That's nonsense, Nicobar. You might as well kill every woman who doesn't please you in bed, or every distiller whose liquor you don't like. Besides, who are you to decide what might give someone else a thrill?"

"It's not a thrill," said Lane. "It's . . . *alien*. It's not something that a human being was ever meant to feel."

"If human beings stuck to what they were meant to feel," said Tchaka, "we wouldn't have any tobacco, or narcotics, or homosexuality, or alcohol. Hell, anything that feels or tastes or sounds or smells good is fair game." He paused for a moment, and then another broad smile crossed his face. "Maybe Tchaka will come out with you and experience this feeling for himself."

"No," said Lane firmly. "This is a battle between me and the creature. I don't need any help."

"Help?" Tchaka laughed. "I'm on the Dreamwish Beast's side, Nicobar!"

"You don't understand what it can do to you," said Lane.

"I can tell you this," said Tchaka. "It wouldn't turn me into a neurotic, bloodthirsty sack of bones. I've heard that ancient royalty on old Earth copulated with sheep and other barnyard animals. Now Tchaka will go them one better and have sex with a ball of energy! Maybe my name will even go down in the history books."

"You're not coming with me, Tchaka," said Lane. "I'm going to pick up that weapon and I'm going to kill the thing and nothing is going to stop me."

"It's like a sex addict killing a woman because he's ashamed of wanting her," said Tchaka. "That damned thing has warped your mind, Nicobar. If it's too much for you, come back to my place. I've even got a virgin for you—that is, if the doctor has finished restoring her."

"Not interested," said Lane.

"It's on the house, Nicobar," said Tchaka. "Who knows? Maybe you learned some new techniques from the Dreamwish Beast."

"Forget it," said Lane.

"Don't tell me you've given up women as well as liquor?" Tchaka laughed.

"All right. I won't tell you."

"I'd sure like to know just what that thing is dishing out," said Tchaka, shaking his head wonderingly. "You're not kidding, are you?"

"No, I'm not."

"If it's *that* potent, I know why you kept after it the past two years."

"Are you through yet?" said Lane. "Can we let it drop now?"

"Not quite," said Tchaka. "Why did you come all the way back to Hellhaven for money? I know for a fact that you've got bank accounts on half a dozen worlds across the galaxy."

"Not any more," said Lane.

"Then buying this weapon will break you?"

Lane nodded. "Just about."

Tchaka snorted. "Thirty years of saving money, and it's all down the drain just like that. You should have been smart and spent it all at Tchaka's, Nicobar."

"I'll make more," said Lane. "After I kill the creature."

"Ah, but what will you spend it on?" said Tchaka. "You've given up women and alcohol, and probably drugs too."

"There are other things to spend money on, Tchaka," said Lane, smiling for the first time.

"Not for men like you and me, Nicobar," said Tchaka. "Not for men who live on the frontier. What would you buy? A house? You live in your spaceship. A library? If books and tapes interested you you wouldn't be here in the first place. Clothes, jewels, trinkets? Who would see them? No, Nicobar, when you live from one minute to the next, as you and I do, you have to spend your money on such things as you can enjoy between those minutes."

"Then I won't spend it," said Lane. "I'll just go back to hunting."

"Why not do that now?"

"I can't," said Lane. "I can't do anything until I kill the creature."

"You keep calling it a thing or a creature," said Tchaka. "I thought it had a name."

"It has a lot of names," said Lane.

"Then why not use one of them?"

"None of them is accurate. It's a creature, plain and simple."

"When will you be going out after it?" asked Tchaka.

"Another two or three days," said Lane. "Whenever the ship is ready. I just sent off the money for the last two components, but I've still got to go to Belore and have it installed in the *Deathmaker*."

"Surely you can come by for one farewell drink before you leave," said Tchaka.

Lane shook his head.

Tchaka shrugged and walked to the door. "R.I.P., my friend. It was very nice to have known you."

"You sound like I'm already dead," said Lane. "The damned creature hasn't killed me yet."

"Look at a mirror, Nicobar," said Tchaka, and left.

CHAPTER
14

The journey from Northpoint to Belore took eighty-three days. Lane spent about four-fifths of the trip in Deepsleep and devoted the remainder of the time to poring over hundreds of star charts until he knew the creature's feeding grounds almost by heart. He tried very hard not to think about the fact that it had just deserted those grounds for the better part of two years.

At last he reached Belore and put the *Deathmaker* down about five miles from the Dornes' shanties. Before he had walked across the intervening distance Vostuvian had come out to greet him.

"You took a long time, killer of animals," said the Dorne in his customary half-whisper.

"I was busy," said Lane.

"And now your business is done?" said Vostuvian.

"No," said Lane. "Now my business is just beginning. Is the weapon ready to install in my ship?"

"It is ready," said Vostuvian. "Are *you*?"

"Yes."

"Good," said the Dorne. "For a time I was afraid you had gone out hunting the Dreamwish Beast with your vibrator. I am glad that I misjudged you."

Lane shot him a quick glance, but couldn't tell whether the remark was an honest or a sardonic one. He walked with Vostuvian in silence for a few moments, then turned to the Dorne. "I went hunting."

"Ah," said Vostuvian. "And did you find it?"

"Yes."

"And are you now convinced that the vibrator will not kill it?"

"Yes," said Lane. "I had six encounters with it."

"Some people take more convincing than others," said Vostuvian, and again Lane could not tell if the comment was straightforward or not.

"What is the effective range of your weapon?" he asked at last.

"Between sixty and seventy thousand miles," said the Dorne. "However, if you could get to within ten or fifteen thousand miles, the drain on your ship's power would be considerably diminished. As it is, we will have to eliminate or bypass most of your ship's nonessential systems. What are your minimum needs in that regard?"

Lane lowered his head in thought for a minute. "Well, I've got to have life support, of course, and food storage."

"Would you consider food recycling?" asked Vostuvian.

"Only as a last resort," said Lane. "My rations are concentrated, and your weapon can't take up that much room."

"Very well," said Vostuvian. "What else will you need?"

"The Deepsleep machine, with two compartments," said Lane.

"Two?"

"One for the Mufti."

"What is a Mufti?" asked Vostuvian.

"Never mind," said Lane. "I need a Deepsleep with two compartments. The Carto-System's built into the main computer, so you couldn't eliminate that even if you wanted to. Ditto for the sensing devices and the navigational computer.

I have a number of star charts I'll want to take along, but they can all be rolled into a large tube. I'll need at least two protective suits, one for space and one for super-hot planets, both with a ten-day supply of oxygen.''

"What else?" asked the Dorne.

"My Dryshower equipment, and that's just about it," said Lane. "And I think I'd better keep one of the ship's weapons operative, just in case your diluter doesn't work."

"Diluter?"

"The entropy weapon," said Lane.

"Which of your own weapons do you wish to retain?"

"The vibrator," said Lane.

"Your laser cannon has a much greater range," said Vostuvian.

"The vibrator," repeated Lane, fighting back a rush of anger.

"As you wish," said Vostuvian. "We will begin adapting the weapon to your ship in the morning."

"What's wrong with right now?" demanded Lane.

"You have waited more than four years, killer of animals," said Vostuvian, "and my people have waited for many millennia. Both of us can wait another day. In the meantime, you will join me for the evening meal. Ondine Gillian assures me that our food is both harmless and nourishing to the human system."

Vostuvian fell silent as he walked toward the shanties, and Lane followed him without a word. They soon reached the ramshackle little dwellings, and before long the Dorne stopped in front of one that seemed no different from the rest, except perhaps that it was even more in need of repair.

"This is my abode," said Vostuvian. "You may enter it if you wish."

"I don't see the weapon anywhere," remarked Lane, looking around the village.

"How big do you think it is?" said Vostuvian, and for the

first time Lane thought he detected just the slightest change of facial expression on the gaunt Dorne.

"I don't know," said Lane, "but I know I sent you a lot of tonnage over the past few years."

"More than ninety percent of it was for use as tools," said Vostuvian, "and what was left was broken down and modified. The weapon is inside my domicile. Come."

Vostuvian entered the shanty, and Lane followed him. The interior didn't differ greatly from the exterior, except for the lack of sunlight. The floor was dirt—or, rather, there was no floor at all. There were two wooden objects which might have been chairs or beds, or perhaps tables. Thrown carelessly on the floor in one corner of the single-room dwelling were numerous tapes and even a pair of books, though Lane couldn't identify the language on the covers.

"We have a community kitchen," whispered Vostuvian. "Your food will be brought here shortly."

"And the diluter?"

Vostuvian walked to a certain section of the floor, brushed aside the dirt, and brought forth a small box that had been buried there. He pulled it out, set it on the ground, and opened it, taking out a compact and very complex piece of machinery that looked more like an ancient meat grinder than anything else.

"That's it?" said Lane incredulously. "That's the whole thing, the weapon that cost me thirty years' savings?"

He reached over, took it from Vostuvian, and hefted it. It was more substantial than it looked, but he was able to lift it with one hand just the same.

"That is your entropy weapon," said Vostuvian.

"It damned well better work," said Lane. "I don't think I could get a two percent return on my investment if I broke it down for parts."

"I thought the only return you were concerned with was the death of the Dreamwish Beast," said Vostuvian.

"What makes you think this little gimmick can kill it?" said Lane, still staring at it.

"It will kill it," said Vostuvian. "With the entirety of your ship's power channeled through it, you will be surprised at what it can do."

"How did your race ever lose the war with these little things in your ships?" asked Lane.

"Because my race only destroyed military targets," said Vostuvian. "Your progenitors were less selective, and when we realized that there was virtually no home world to return to, we surrendered."

"That's not quite the way I remember it from my history books," said Lane.

"History is written by the victors," said Vostuvian emotionlessly.

"Perhaps," said Lane. "But I seem to recall a little encounter called the Battle of Sirius V, in which a handful of our ships decimated the bulk of your fleet."

"Indeed they did," said Vostuvian. "But they did so under a flag of truce."

"I don't recall it that way," said Lane. "And since there were no Dorne survivors, I think I might be allowed to question the authenticity of your version."

"Question it all you wish," said Vostuvian. "Are you here to reawaken old hostilities, or to arm yourself for new ones?"

Lane glared at the Dorne for a long moment, then shrugged and went back to examining the diluter.

"Where will the firing mechanism be?" he asked at last.

"Anywhere you wish. Since you won't be using your laser cannon, we can hook it up there, modify the tracking and locking mechanisms, and tie it in to your main power output."

"If you know how to do that, why have your people lost the secret of space flight?" said Lane sharply.

"We haven't lost the secret," said Vostuvian. "Only the economy and the desire. You find it inconceivable that I should be content to sit here on my home world, awaiting the death of my race. I find it equally inconceivable that you have spent the bulk of your adult life flying all around the galaxy, hastening the death of other races. Which life-style is more in harmony with the nature of things?"

"I never thought it was the nature of things—or at least of thinking things—to squat in the dirt and contemplate their own deaths without lifting a finger to fend off their fates," said Lane. "And, in case you've forgotten, it was the Dornes who tried to exterminate the Dreamwish Beasts, and it was you yourself who wanted to come along with me while I hunt down the last of them."

Vostuvian was about to answer him when another Dorne entered the shanty, placed two trays of food on the ground, and left. Lane, who hadn't eaten for about twenty hours, sat down on the dirt and examined the contents of the nearer tray. It consisted of a number of desert vegetables, most of them resembling red-hued cacti, and a piece of meat, which was somewhere between an eel and a snake but very definitely not of either immediate family.

"Do you have any eating implements?" Lane asked Vostuvian.

"Fingers and teeth have always sufficed," replied the Dorne.

Lane shrugged. He'd been forced to eat some pretty unappetizing meals on various other worlds, and the lack of silverware bothered him less than it would have bothered most people. He reached out, grabbed the meat, and brought it toward his mouth.

It wriggled.

"Is this damned thing alive?" he asked, holding it up for Vostuvian to see.

"No," said the Dorne. "Its muscular fiber is such that it approximates independent motion even after being cut and cooked. I assure you it is quite dead."

"It better be," muttered Lane, staring at it.

"We rather like it this way," said Vostuvian, taking an enormous bite of his own meat.

Lane watched the Dorne wolf down the meat in unchewed chunks, not unlike a large carnivore, and decided to do the same. He soon understood why Vostuvian hadn't masticated. It was the toughest, least-cooked hunk of meat he'd ever tasted. Just tearing off a piece between his teeth was a major effort, and he found that the primary purpose in cooking it at all was to immerse it in enough greasy juices so that the oversized chunk would slide down his throat without too much difficulty. He tried to categorize the animal by its taste, but was unable to do so, which may have been for the best; he concluded that he would like it better—or dislike it less— if he remained ignorant of its origins.

He took two more huge bites of the meat, decided that it wasn't worth the effort, and concentrated on nibbling the cactus without cutting his tongue to ribbons. He'd had worse meals, many of them, but he nonetheless began thinking very fondly of his food concentrates back at the *Deathmaker*.

When the repast was finished he leaned back, belched twice, and pushed the tray aside.

"Did you like it?" asked Vostuvian.

"About as much as you'd like a well-done steak, I imagine," replied Lane. "Am I to sleep here tonight, or back at my ship?"

"Whichever you prefer," said Vostuvian. "Where will you begin your search for the Dreamwish Beast?"

"Somewhere between Alphard and Canphor," replied Lane. "I have enough fuel for three years. That ought to be more than sufficient."

"I hope so," said Vostuvian.

"Why wouldn't it be?" said Lane.

"In the past, Dreamwish Beasts have been known to leave the dust cloud for even longer periods of time."

"Perhaps," said Lane. "But whether or not it's intelligent, it *is* a creature of habit. I don't think it will leave unless it's running away from me—or after me—and in either case I'll have a clear shot at it. Which leads me to another question: just how many times can I fire the diluter without completely draining the *Deathmaker*'s power reserves?"

"Three times, perhaps four," said Vostuvian. "Do you plan to miss?"

"I never miss."

"Then you shall fire it only once," said the Dorne.

"I like to know all my capabilities before I go on a hunt," said Lane. "Any objections?"

"None at all," whispered Vostuvian. "I just assumed, killer of animals, that—"

"Another thing," interrupted Lane. "My name is Lane, not killer of animals. If you want to address me, use my name."

"As you wish, Lane," said Vostuvian.

"Another question: When I fire the diluter, what will happen to my ship's systems?"

"I will set up the circuitry so that the life-support system will remain unaffected," said the Dorne. "The other systems will go dead for the duration of the firing time, and perhaps even a little beyond that."

"What's the maximum time I can keep the diluter working without burning out all the circuits?" asked Lane.

"Ten seconds, perhaps eleven," said Vostuvian. "It will take about eight seconds to kill the Dreamwish Beast, so if I were you, Lane, I would aim very carefully."

"I'll take it under advisement," said Lane dryly.

"Three years may not be enough time in which to kill the Dreamwish Beast," said Vostuvian after a long silence.

"Then I'll take four years, or ten, or fifty."

"It will take less time with me than without me," said Vostuvian.

"No," said Lane.

"You are being impractical, Lane," said the Dorne.

"Vostuvian, I don't like you very much right now. I would like you even less if we were cooped up together in the ship for any length of time."

"Are you looking for comradery, or hunting the Dreamwish Beast?" said Vostuvian.

"The two are not mutually exclusive," said Lane. "I have the Mufti for companionship, and the creature for a quarry."

"Nonetheless, you would hunt it more efficiently if you took me along," said the Dorne.

"I'm already efficient," said Lane. "Why should I let you come along?"

"To make sure you fire the diluter and not the vibrator," said Vostuvian.

Lane was on his feet in a second. Another second saw the two empty trays flying across the room, barely missing Vostuvian's head. Lane stormed over to the Dorne and a powerful hand shot out, grabbing Vostuvian's incredibly slender neck and shaking it.

"If you ever say anything like that again," rasped Lane between clenched teeth, "the race of Dorne is going to be extinct even sooner than you expected. Understand?"

Vostuvian made no attempt to answer him, or even to nod his head. He stood stock-still, eyes closed, not breathing. For a minute Lane thought he had killed him, but when he relaxed his grip and stepped back the Dorne opened his eyes as if nothing had happened.

"If I were you, I would save my anger for the Dreamwish Beast," said Vostuvian in a hoarse whisper.

"I've got a lot of it to spare," said Lane coldly.

"I am aware of that," said the Dorne, gently stroking his neck. "Have you ever asked yourself why?"

"Never," said Lane. "Now, have you got anything else to say before I go back to my ship?"

"Only a question," said Vostuvian. "As I mentioned once before, the Dreamwish Beast will not approach your ship once the entropy weapon is installed. What will you do when you cannot find it?"

"I'll worry about that problem if and when it arises," said Lane. "Anything else?"

"No."

"Good. Be at the *Deathmaker* at sunrise and get the hell off the premises as soon as you're through working."

Then he was outside, walking back to his ship, and vaguely wondering when and where he had acquired a temper.

CHAPTER
15

Time was running out.

Lane had been in space for thirty-two Standard months without sighting the creature. He estimated that he had perhaps five months' worth of fuel remaining, and even less food and water.

It had been a hideously frustrating trip thus far. He couldn't take a Deepsleep, for fear of missing the creature. He couldn't land on a planet, for fear of using up too much fuel. He couldn't even be sure his diluter worked; its potency was so ephemeral that it could be tested only in battle.

And, of course, the major frustration was the absence of the creature. Before he had installed the diluter into his ship, it had followed him all over the galaxy, bringing forth that dark, secret self that lived deep inside of him. Now that he was ready to do battle, the creature was well-nigh impossible to find.

And time, he knew, was not all that was running out. There was no money left to pay for the fuel and supplies he would soon need.

Lane checked his star charts again, examining those options that still remained. He could continue searching the dust cloud for another three months, but then the only known source of work and/or money within the *Deathmaker*'s range would be William Campbell Blessbull XXIII, and his lawsuit against Blessbull was still in the courts. On the other hand, if he diverted now, he could make it to the Deluros system with a few days' fuel to spare—and, while he hadn't done any work for the Vainmill Syndicate in almost eight years, at least they had nothing against him.

His decision made, Lane left the dust cloud and set out for Deluros VIII, the capital world of the race of Man, the cultural, political, financial, and military epicenter of humanity. Man had long since outgrown Earth, and while he viewed his birthplace with an almost religious devotion, he had moved his government lock, stock, and barrel to the Deluros system, which was more centrally located and had one of those rare worlds that possessed Earthlike conditions while boasting ten times its surface area.

Even this proved inadequate to man's needs, and Deluros VI, another oxygen world, had been broken up into forty-eight planetoids, each of them housing some huge-domed governmental agency or department. The military had immediately taken over four of the worldlets and was already cramped for room.

But the planetoids were merely the backstage area of the Deluros system. It was Deluros VIII, that shining, temperate blue-and-gold-and-green world, that possessed the power to act and to lead. As Lane approached it, he was ordered to assume orbit and then to enter one of the literally hundreds of thousands of planet-circling hangars and refueling stations. He did as he was instructed, leaving the *Deathmaker* snugly ensconced in one of the stations, and boarded a shuttle flight for the surface.

He had seen pictures and paintings of Deluros VIII and talked to people who had lived and visited there, but no second- or third-hand descriptions could adequately have prepared him for the enormous world. He had often wondered why no inhabitant of Deluros VIII had ever evinced any sectionalism or nationalism. Now he knew.

The surface area of the planet was covered by one gigantic megalopolis. There were parks and farms and lakes and even a pair of deserts, but snaking through all of them was the city. It sprawled, shiny and new—for most of it was less than a millennium old, and all of it was in a state of constant repair and refurbishment—stretching huge metal and plastic and cement tentacles in every direction, covering both polar areas and even burrowing beneath the oceans. The structures, which could just as easily have been coldly and impersonally functional, highlighted the current culmination of the architect's art. Where Lodin XI had been completely incomprehensible to him, this world, even from a height of forty miles, seemed sensible to the nth degree. Huge, broad thoroughfares followed the paths of least resistance from one section of the planet-city to another, monorails encircled large, densely populated sections of the city, industrial complexes seemed to be clustered together, and everything had a familiar, if enlarged, feel to it.

The shuttle landed in what seemed a combination airport/spaceport/monorail terminal, and the passengers were informed that they could now make connections for any sector of the planet they wished to visit. If, on the other hand, they had business with a governmental agency, it would behoove them to first determine whether that business could be transacted here, or whether they would have to go to one of the Deluros VI planetoids.

Lane walked over to a computerized directory and requested the address of Ector Allsworth. He was informed that Allsworth no longer maintained a permanent residence on Deluros VIII, but had been planetbound for almost a week. His exact whereabouts were unknown.

Lane then tried the Vainmill Syndicate, but ran into so much front-office red tape when he contacted them via videophone that he gave up the effort to hunt Allsworth down through his corporation.

Finally, on a hunch, he fed the name of Ilse Vescott into the computer, which spat it back out almost instantly along with a small red CLASSIFIED notice. Lane knew enough not to persist.

His next stop was a local newstape office, where he searched through the social and financial sections until he found a female reporter who had mentioned Vescott thrice in a month. He sought out the woman, bribed her with half of his last four thousand Maria Theresa dollars, and went to the address given him. Fortunately, it wasn't halfway around the planet, and his transportation for the two-hundred-mile journey left him with most of his remaining money intact.

That afternoon he approached Ilse Vescott's house on foot. The structure, set almost a mile back from the thoroughfare and looking out over a perfectly manicured lawn of mutated, light-blue grass that was dotted here and there with formal gardens, was more palace than house, more sumptuous hotel than private dwelling place. Lane estimated it to have fully three hundred rooms, each the size of a normal house. It stood fifteen stories high, was smooth, sleek and shiny, and had about it the atmosphere of an impregnable fortress.

If he felt uneasy about presenting himself in his standard hunting togs—the only type of clothing he had worn for years—he made no show of it. He walked to the head of the huge, belted driveway, stepped onto it, and was quickly transported to the main entrance of the mansion.

The ornate door opened silently and he stepped into an obsidian foyer. There were numerous doors leading into the interior of the house, but all were closed.

"I am the completely automated Spy-Eye Security System," said a metallic voice. "Please state your name and business here."

"Nicobar Lane, killer."

"I have no record of a Nicobar Lane," said the voice. "Do you have an appointment?"

"Some security system!" snorted Lane. "Tell Ilse Vescott that she's got a killer in her house."

"You have not answered my question," said the Spy-Eye System. "Have you an appointment?"

"Absolutely," said Lane. "Now let me in."

"I have no record of such an appointment," said the voice.

And suddenly the foyer echoed with a peal of high-pitched feminine laughter.

"This is absolutely priceless!" said the voice, still laughing. "Come in, Mr. Lane. The fifth door on your right."

Lane walked to the door, opened it, and stepped into a room that, at a conservative estimate, had cost twice the price of the *Deathmaker* to furnish. The floor was covered by a white, fluffy carpet made of the pelts and heads of literally thousands of tiny arctic animals, each approximately the size of the Mufti. The walls and ceiling were covered with mirrors—but they were mirrors with a difference, each shaped so as to give a totally different and mind-bending picture of the room repeated to infinity. Chairs and tables of baroque design filled the room, each composed of gold or platinum and inlaid with jewels of a type Lane had never seen. And at the far end of the enormous chamber was a Bafflediver. Its hide had been encrusted with glowing and glistening jewels, and its enormous, bafflelike snout had been hollowed out to form a cushioned chair.

On—or in—the chair sat Ilse Vescott. At first glance he concluded that she was one of the most beautiful women he had ever seen, but as he walked closer he began revising his opinion. She wore a low-cut, skin-tight, and very revealing one-piece suit in the haute-couture fashion of the moment, and something struck him as being very wrong. That skin, displayed in such quantity, was too perfect, too free from blemishes. Not even plastic rejuvenation treatments could do that.

. His gaze rose to her face. It, too, was flawless, though the eyes were perhaps set a little too deeply into her head—and then, as he got within a few feet of her, he knew why. Her face, like her body, was synthetic, composed of perfectly textured fibers, molded by a medical sculptor who had captured the true essence of beauty and sensuality in a single subject. Only the eyes—old and hard and aloof—belonged to Ilse Vescott, and even the magician who had given her the body and face of a modern Venus had been unable to totally hide or change them.

Lane forced himself to stop staring, then gestured to the foyer. "How much did that thing cost you?"

"The security system?" she asked, and the warm, red, artificial lips broke into a smile. "A little over two hundred thousand credits. Why?"

"For that much money, someone should have put the word 'killer' into its vocabulary banks. I've got a pet that cost me the equivalent of twenty credits who can give you better protection."

"I admire your audacity, Mr. Lane," she said, rising and extending her hand to him. It felt firm, vibrant—and cold. "Who is it that you've come to kill?"

"No one," said Lane. "I kill animals, not people."

"How quaint," she said. She touched a jewel on one of her bracelets and a bar rose from the floor, its sides covered with the same white pelts that made up the carpet. "May I offer you a drink before you relate your adventures of derring-do?"

Lane nodded, and she opened a tall thin bottle, pouring its contents into two crystal glasses. Lane took a sip, decided that he liked it, and downed it with a single swallow. Ilse Vescott sipped hers slowly.

"Very good," said Lane.

"Should I know who you are, Mr. Lane?" she asked at last.

"Probably not," said Lane. "My dealings, such as they are, have been with Ector Allsworth."

"Ah! Then you must work for the Vainmill Syndicate."

"I work for me," said Lane.

"A subtle distinction," said Ilse Vescott. "And why have you come to see me?"

"Because I couldn't find Allsworth. I know he's on the planet, and your house seemed the most likely place. Is he here?"

"Yes, but he's such a *bore*," she said, wrinkling her artificial nose and pursing her synthetic lips. "Besides, he's just a hireling. I own him, just as I own Vainmill and this house and everything else you see around you."

"That's a lot for one person to own," said Lane.

"I'm a very unusual person," said Ilse Vescott, her ancient eyes staring out at him with detached amusement. "And I like to own things. Don't you?"

"I don't own things," said Lane. "I kill them."

"And just what are you interested in killing, Mr. Lane?"

"The Dreamwish Beast."

"What a fabulous name!" she exclaimed. "It conjures up all kinds of exotic pictures. What is it like?"

"Like nothing else in the universe," said Lane.

"Is it very beautiful?"

"Very," said Lane. "It's like . . . like a living star. It pulses and throbs with energy, and glows with life. It lives in space; it was born there and it will die there."

"What does it breathe?" she asked.

"It doesn't."

"Then how will you know when it's dead?"

"I'll know," said Lane grimly.

"I always thought professional hunters were supposed to

be cold and dispassionate," said Ilse. "Suddenly you look like this thing is your mortal enemy."

"Its beauty is only half of it," said Lane. "It's a powerful, dangerous, maleficent life form."

"Shades of Dr. Jekyll and Mr. Hyde!" Ilse laughed. "Tell me more about it."

"It's the last of its kind. Once there were more of them, but they were all killed off eons ago. This one survived."

"If it's the last of its species, maybe you should try to capture it instead," said Ilse.

"It can't be captured," said Lane. "It can only be destroyed."

"What color is it?"

"It changes," said Lane. "Sometimes it's red, sometimes it's almost yellow. It depends on how fast it's moving, and what it's feeling at the moment."

"How can anyone possibly tell what a creature like that is feeling?" said Ilse.

"Just an expression," said Lane, suddenly tense. "Allsworth's been after me for years to kill it. I'm ready to do so now."

"Surely you didn't come all the way to Deluros just to tell us that," she said.

"I came to talk price."

"Ah. And how much do you plan to ask for your services?"

"Half a million credits, or its equivalent in some other form of currency."

"That's a lot of money, even for something so wondrous as a Dreamwish Beast," said Ilse.

"Not to you it isn't," said Lane. "And that's what it will take."

"It appears I am going to need Ector's advice after all," said Ilse, removing a cushion from the arm of her Bafflediver-chair and pressing one of a number of buttons that were revealed.

A moment later Allsworth entered the room, still gray of skin and yellow of eye, a little portlier and balder than when Lane had first met him. He stared at Lane for a long minute before identifying him.

"Lane?" he asked tentatively.

Lane nodded and extended his hand.

"You've aged," said Allsworth. "What are you doing in the Deluros system?"

"Mr. Lane has volunteered to slay the Dreamwish Beast for us," said Ilse. "What do you think of that, Ector?"

"I thought you told me that it was just a myth," said Allsworth.

"I was wrong," said Lane.

"Ector," said Ilse, "how much will we pay Mr. Lane for delivering a Dreamwish Beast to one of our museums?"

"How much does he want?" asked Allsworth.

"Half a million credits," said Ilse.

"Sign him to a contract immediately," said Allsworth. He turned to Lane. "Why so cheap? You know as well as I do how much it's worth."

"There's a condition," said Lane.

"Oh?" said Allsworth.

"I want it in advance."

"I thought so!" said Allsworth. "Do you want to just walk out of here quietly and peacefully, or shall I have you thrown out?"

"What's the matter, Ector?" said Ilse.

"Look at him, Ilse," said Allsworth, moving to her side. "Look at his eyes, his hands. He hasn't filled a contract in years, for us or for anyone else. How old would you say he is?"

Ilse Vescott looked at the thinning white hair, the gaunt,

hollow face, the wrinkled clawlike hands. "In his nineties, at least."

"How old are you, Lane?" said Allsworth.

"None of your business," said Lane. "Is it a deal or isn't it?"

"He's on something," said Allsworth. "Can't you see he's an addict?"

"What a pity," said Ilse sadly. "And you made it sound so real."

"It *is* real," said Lane. "It's out there, and I've got the only weapon that can kill it."

"The only thing he's got is some habit that needs feeding," said Allsworth. "Let me throw him out of here, Ilse."

"In a minute," said Ilse distractedly. Then she turned back to Lane. "Tell me more about it, Mr. Lane."

"There's not much more to tell," said Lane. "It lives, and it feeds, and it flies, and it can be destroyed—if you'll pay me to do it."

"What will you put up for collateral?" asked Ilse.

"You're not going to give him any money, are you?" demanded Allsworth.

"Do be quiet, Ector," said Ilse. "This animal has fired my imagination. If Vainmill isn't interested, I'll commission it myself. What is your collateral, Mr. Lane?"

"Everything I own," said Lane.

"Everything," repeated Ilse. "That's a lot to put up."

"It used to be more," said Lane wryly. "Right now it consists of my ship and my weapon."

"Half a million credits is too much to spend on a fancy, Mr. Lane," said Ilse. "Even one as delightful as yours. I'll advance you fifty thousand credits. Take it or leave it."

"I'll take it," said Lane without hesitation.

"Ector will accompany you to your ship," said Ilse. "You can turn over the papers to him then."

"He's robbing you blind, Ilse!" protested Allsworth. "You'll never see him again."

"Perhaps," said Ilse, pouring herself another drink.

"Then why are you doing it?"

"Because it amuses me," she said. "Or, if you'd rather, call it the sympathy of a lovely young woman for an old man who's long past his prime."

And Lane, staring at the ancient eyes that were surrounded by those perfect synthetic features, couldn't tell which of the two was her real reason.

Nor, now that he was going to get fuel for his ship, did he particularly care.

CHAPTER
16

The *Deathmaker* departed the Deluros system while Lane tried to decide what to do next. Fifty thousand credits could keep the ship going at near maximum speed for a decade or a century or all eternity—provided that he didn't have to maneuver. Once in free flight, the *Deathmaker*'s inertia was all that was required to keep it going at a constant speed; but every time he slowed down, or increased his speed, or changed his angle of flight, he used fuel. And, even with the money Ilse Vescott had given him, fuel would continue to be at a premium once he began chasing the creature in earnest.

So, while he had bought himself a little time, he hadn't necessarily bought the means to catch the creature. He needed still more money, and he wasn't quite sure how to go about getting it. His first thought was to find a fueling station on some frontier world and take what he needed at gunpoint, but he immediately discarded the notion; he'd have every police agency in the area looking for the *Deathmaker*, and he didn't need that kind of problem during the final phase of the hunt.

So he looked at his other options. It had been so many years since he'd delivered on a contract, or even accepted one, that it wasn't too likely he could go back to hunting—

nor did he want to. That would eat up too much time, even if he succeeded in obtaining work.

Of course, he could always hunt illegal or prohibited species. Some of them, like the Bellringer of Daedalus VII, or old Earth's last remaining wild animal, the dingo, brought pretty substantial prices from private collectors, and he had absolute confidence in his ability to hunt down any animal ever born, whelped, foaled, or hatched. But, while the pay was better, the objection was the same as to hunting legitimate prey: the time factor, which would be increased by the need for secrecy and for personal delivery of the carcasses. Besides, he'd been out of touch for so long that he no longer knew which species were on the protected list.

He briefly contemplated making a raid on the fortress world of Braxton IV, where the Democracy harvested mionate, the most powerful drug yet known to man, but he wrote it off as being too long a shot. Besides, even if he succeeded where countless others had failed, he needed money, not unprocessed mionate—and he didn't know how or where to convert the latter into the former without bringing the Democracy's policing agencies down on his head.

He even toyed with the notion of returning to Deluros VIII and either robbing or kidnapping Ilse Vescott. He rejected that thought quickly, not on any moral grounds, but simply because the chances of success were so slim.

He pored over his possibilities for hours, and when he had eliminated the impossible and the improbable, he sorted out what remained. He did it coldly, efficiently, estimating risks and profits, matching methods against each other. When he was through he knew exactly what he had to do in order to get sufficient fuel to be sure of catching the creature. For what lay ahead of him, he felt no moral repugnance; he merely considered it an unpleasant necessity to be gotten over with as quickly as possible.

He switched on the Carto-System, tied it in to the navigational computer and the main computer's memory banks, and got a listing of all those worlds that had been opened up in the past decade. He then eliminated all those which were agricultural colonies; they wouldn't have enough money or convertible goods to make the risk worthwhile. He was especially interested in those planets that had been settled by religious and/or pacifistic groups, those whose defenses could reasonably be assumed to be minimal or even nonexistent.

To this list he added some of the frontier mining worlds which he knew to have almost fully automated operations, overseen by at most a handful of men, and ideally by just one or two.

Then he computed his fuel to the last cubic millimeter, laid in a course that would take him away from both Northpoint and the dust cloud but would leave him enough fuel to return to Northpoint at the end of his voyage, estimated how many times he could land, and selected those worlds on which he would set the *Deathmaker* down.

And, with the emotionless efficiency that had characterized his preparations so many times in the past, Nicobar Lane planned his next-to-last hunt.

CHAPTER
17

Tchaka walked through a maze of rooms and levels until he came to his private quarters. He debated having a pair of his girls come in with him, but he decided that he was too sleepy to do them justice. He opened the door, turned on the lights, and froze.

"Nicobar!" he finally exclaimed.

"Shut the door," said Lane, not moving from the comfortable form-fitting chair in which he reclined.

"It's been years!" said Tchaka. "Did you finally kill your monster?"

"Not quite," said Lane.

"I hadn't expected to see you until you had destroyed it," said Tchaka. "To what do I owe the honor of this visit?"

"You're a fence, Tchaka," said Lane. Tchaka opened his mouth to object but Lane waved him down. "Don't deny it. I'm not here to arrest you. I've got a batch of stuff to unload."

Tchaka closed the door behind him.

"I thought you were just about destitute, Nicobar," he said. "What do you have to sell?"

Lane picked up a large bag he had placed behind his chair, walked over to a bed-table, and emptied out the contents.

There were rings of every imaginable variety and value, necklaces, timepieces, even a few platinum teeth.

"Where did you get all of this, Nicobar?" asked Tchaka, examining a large bracelet.

"A rich uncle died," said Lane.

"Yours?" Tchaka grinned.

"What difference does it make?" said Lane.

"I heard that a bunch of religious freaks—what were they called? Ah! The Roanoke Colony—had been robbed and murdered. The newstapes say it was done with a screecher. And then there were the miners out on Bastion, and . . ."

"Don't waste your breath," said Lane coldly. "I never keep up with the newstapes. They don't interest me."

"Did you kill them, Nicobar?"

"Did you take over this business by killing Horatio Constantine?" said Lane.

"Serves me right for asking a personal question." Tchaka grinned. "The subject is closed."

"Good."

"However, you will allow me to ask you why you're here when the Dreamwish Beast is out there."

"I need more money," said Lane.

"I thought you had enough to build your weapon years ago," said Tchaka.

"It's built. I need more fuel for the *Deathmaker*."

"How much more?"

"Half a million credits' worth."

"I don't deal in credits," said Tchaka. "You know that."

"Its equivalent, then," said Lane.

Tchaka looked over Lane's haul again. "Three hundred thousand, tops," he said at last.

"Who are you kidding, Tchaka?" said Lane. "That stuff's worth a good three million, even on the black market."

Tchaka shook his head. "Whoever wiped out the miners on Bastion also knocked off two members of the Democracy's

Bureau of Mineralogy. Their agents have been to visit me twice already. I'm going to have to sit on this stuff for years before I can push it. Sloppy worker, that Bastion killer. A complete amateur.''

"Four hundred thousand," said Lane. "That's the least I can take."

Tchaka shook his head. "No, Nicobar. Three hundred."

He suddenly found himself staring into the business end of a screecher.

"I'm not kidding, Tchaka," said Lane. "I need that money. You're going to make a six hundred percent profit as it is; don't throw your life away trying for a higher percentage."

"You look like you'd really use that thing, Nicobar," said Tchaka, standing stock-still.

"I'll do what I have to do," said Lane. "I've got to fuel up the *Deathmaker*."

"Three hundred thousand, four hundred thousand, what difference does it make?" said Tchaka. "You're going to be swimming around in fuel either way."

"I'm not coming back this time until I kill it," said Lane. "However long it takes, wherever the creature goes, whatever it does, I'm going to get the job done."

"I don't like what this thing has done to you, Nicobar," said Tchaka. "I thought we were friends."

"I don't like what it's done to me either," said Lane. "That's why it has to die."

"Just remember that you want to kill *it* and not me," said Tchaka. "Put your weapon away, Nicobar."

"You'll pay me four hundred thousand?"

"Yes."

"And give me your word that you won't try to rip me apart?"

"Freely given," said Tchaka. Lane put the screecher back in his belt, and Tchaka poured himself a glass of Aldebaranian absinthe. "Still a teetotaler?"

Lane nodded.

"How long has it been since you've had a woman, Nicobar?"

"Don't start, Tchaka," said Lane.

"All right." Tchaka shrugged. "I'll get the money for you in the morning. It'll have to be in cash, though; I want no record of any financial dealings with you. Anyone dumb enough to kill two government agents had to leave clues behind."

Lane ignored the statement. "I'll be by for it at sunrise."

"Whenever you wish," said Tchaka. "By the way, what makes you so sure you're going to find the monster this time, Nicobar? You've been chasing after it for years and years."

"I'll find it," Lane said savagely.

"That's what you said last time," Tchaka pointed out.

"Last time I was wrong. This time I'm not. I'll have enough fuel to keep the *Deathmaker* in space the rest of my life if need be. I know more about the creature than anyone else alive. And I want to kill it more than any man ever wanted anything."

"We always kill the things we love," said Tchaka.

Lane's eyes blazed for a moment, and Tchaka thought he was going to pull out the screecher again; but slowly, by dint of almost visible effort, the hunter forced his rage to subside. "You will never say that or anything like that again," he said so softly that Tchaka had difficulty hearing him. "Do you understand?"

"Whatever you say, Nicobar," said Tchaka. "But you must understand that you have become a very frustrating man to try to talk with."

"You won't have to worry about it much longer," said Lane. "I'm leaving as soon as my ship is ready."

"I have the feeling that this is the last time I'll ever see you," said Tchaka.

"You'll live," said Lane.

"Ah, but will you?" said Tchaka. "I come originally from Abilla III. We're not exactly mutants, but we've undergone a few changes over the millennia. For instance, I have every reason to expect my vitality and virility to continue undiminished for another forty or fifty years. But what about you, Nicobar? You look like you've got one foot in the grave already. You're an old man. What makes you think you'll live long enough to kill your Dreamwish Beast?"

"Because I hate it too much to die before it does," said Lane. "However long it takes, I'll keep alive one way or another."

Tchaka shook his head. "Hatred's a frail thing to depend on for nourishment—especially a hatred that's as poorly constructed as yours. If it was Tchaka, he wouldn't waste the rest of his life on hatred. Lust, maybe, or love, or even hunger. That might keep Tchaka going. But hatred? Never. It's not worth the effort."

"No one is asking you to make the effort," said Lane.

"True," agreed Tchaka. "But then, no one asked you to make it either."

"I have to," said Lane softly. "It can never be allowed to do to anyone else what it has done to me."

"I'm glad to know that's an altruistic statement," said Tchaka, "because it sure as hell might sound like jealousy or possessiveness to the uninitiated."

Without word or warning Lane reached for his screecher, but Tchaka was faster and grabbed his arm before he could withdraw the weapon. The huge man disarmed Lane, gave him a mighty backhand slap, and then walked back to where he had been standing.

"That was stupid, Nicobar," said Tchaka disgustedly. "Just plain stupid. If you kill me, who will give you your money?"

Lane glared at him, sullenly and silently.

"Look," continued Tchaka, "if it'll make you any easier

to get along with, I hope you kill the goddamn thing. I hope you chop it up into little pieces and make each piece suffer the agonies of everlasting perdition. I really do. Mostly, though, I hope you'll stop trying to kill me every time I mention the blasted monster. Whatever it's done to you, just keep telling yourself that it's not Tchaka's fault. You've got a real thing about it, Nicobar. One minute you're as calm and logical as ever, and then you start talking about the damned creature and suddenly you're a homicidal maniac. You should have stuck to liquor and women, Nicobar; they feel just as good and they don't warp your brain. Look at me: I want a woman right now every bit as much as you want your Dreamwish Beast, maybe even more. But I don't go into a killing rage because of it."

"Just give me my money and let me go," said Lane.

"I can't," said Tchaka. "Not until morning. You know I don't keep that kind of cash on hand here. You'll get your money, never fear."

"And my screecher."

"You'll get that too," said Tchaka. "I'll have it placed on your ship. You can hunt it up once you've taken off."

Lane stood up and walked to the door.

"One last thing, Nicobar," said Tchaka.

"What?"

"How long have you been chasing the Dreamwish Beast?"

"A long time."

"What do you plan to do after you catch it?"

"I've already told you," said Lane. "I commissioned a weapon that utilizes the entropy principle. Once I get the creature in my sights, the weapon will simply dissipate it."

"You don't understand me," said Tchaka. "That's what you're going to do *when* you catch it."

"What the hell are you talking about?" said Lane.

"You've used up all your money and all your youth," said

Tchaka. "You're probably being hunted for murder at this very moment. You've reneged on so many contracts that it's doubtful you'll ever be able to set up shop as a hunter again. So I repeat: What are you going to do *after* you catch it?"

Lane stared uncomprehendingly at him for a full minute, then turned and walked out the door.

CHAPTER
18

The *Deathmaker* had one last stop to make.

Lane put the ship down less than a mile from the Dorne village. There was no need for secrecy; by the time the police traced him here he'd be long gone.

He allowed the Mufti to cling to his shoulder as he walked the short distance to the row of dilapidated shanties. It was very cold now that the sun had set, and he hastened his pace.

When he reached the village he found that he couldn't remember which hut was Vostuvian's, so he stood at the midpoint of the single row of dwellings and called the Dorne by name.

A moment later Vostuvian emerged, expressionless as ever.

"I knew you would come back," he said in his now-familiar half-whisper.

"Do you still want to go?" said Lane.

"Yes."

"Then get as much concentrated food as you can beg, borrow, or steal, or prepare to spend the entire hunt eating what I eat."

"We have no concentrated foodstuffs," said Vostuvian.

"All right," said Lane. "Round up enough food to last you for a week or two, until your system gets used to a steady diet of my stuff. Will you need anything else?" He could not resist getting the dig in: "Clean rags, for instance?"

"What I am wearing will be quite sufficient," said Vostuvian.

"Good. I'll give you two hours to hunt up your food and say your good-byes."

"May I ask what has brought about this change, Lane?" said the Dorne. "As I said, I knew that you would come back for me, but I didn't expect you this soon."

"No choice," said Lane. "There is very likely a warrant out for my arrest, and if there isn't, there soon will be. I have enough fuel and money to run the *Deathmaker* for the rest of our lives and then some, and it stands to reason that if I'm ever going to need you, I'd better get you aboard now. It won't take the police very long to figure out that I've been here a couple of times on business."

"Why are the authorities after you?" asked Vostuvian.

"They think I've graduated from a killer of animals to a killer of men."

"And have you?" asked Vostuvian.

"Does it make any difference to you, as long as I take you along on the hunt?"

Vostuvian closed his eyes and stood rigid and unbreathing for a moment. Then he looked up. "No, Lane, it makes no difference at all. The only killing that concerns me is that which lies ahead."

"Good," said Lane. "Should you bring along any tools to repair the diluter if it goes on the blink?"

"On the blink?" repeated the Dorne.

"Breaks down."

"It will not break down, Lane. As long as your ship runs, the entropy weapon will function."

"Good enough," said Lane. "I'll have to take your word for it. Go scare up your food and get back here as fast as you can."

The Dorne disappeared into the darkness, in what Lane assumed was the direction of the community kitchen. The hunter leaned against the shanty to wait for Vostuvian's return, his eyes scanning the heavens. He wondered where the creature was at that very instant, whether it was gliding through space or feeding off the dust cloud, or perhaps waiting for the *Deathmaker*. It had been a long time since he'd seen it, but he could still feel the sensations—the hatred, the fear, and those other, darker emotions—as if he had just experienced them minutes ago. He knew he'd feel the apprehension again, cascading over him in irresistible waves—but this time things would be different. This time he was ready for it, ready and armed and eager to get on with the hunt.

His concentration was broken as the Mufti began jabbering insanely and launched itself toward the ground. A moment later it waddled back to him, a huge golden-backed beetle carried proudly in its mouth. It played with the insect for a while, and when the beetle finally expired it tossed the tiny carcass into the air, catching and swallowing it on the way down. A moment later it was back on Lane's shoulder again, but this time its entire body was tense as it scanned the ground for another late-night snack.

Lane turned his head and stared at his strange little pet as best he could. If the Mufti had a redeeming social virtue he had yet to discover it, and yet he was strangely attached to the maniacal creature. He found its chattering and gibbering a comfort during his long months in deep space, and felt a certain warmth in the knowledge that the Mufti stayed with him by choice. There had been hundreds of times on a multitude of worlds that the little animal could have gone off and left him if it had so desired, but it never evinced any interest in doing so. He was about to give its head a friendly pat when it shrieked like the idiot he suspected it was, dove to the ground again, and a moment later was munching happily on another beetle.

They remained in the cool darkness, man and Mufti, for the better part of an hour. Then Vostuvian returned with a foul-smelling sack slung carelessly over his shoulder, and they walked to the *Deathmaker*.

A moment later Belore was a globe of ever-decreasing size in the viewscreen, and Lane, after many years and many false starts, began the final hunt of his career.

CHAPTER
19

Vostuvian set up housekeeping in a corner of the pilot's cabin. The Dorne put in his time acquainting himself with the control and instrument panels, but otherwise never willingly crossed the imaginary line around his quarters. He refused to use the Dryshower until Lane made it a use-it-or-get-off-the-ship proposition, and his two-week supply of odoriferous food turned out to be a two-month supply instead. The fact that it had rotted and stunk to high heaven long before the two months were up didn't seem to bother him in the least.

As for Lane, he spent most of his waking hours at the instrument panels, searching vainly for some sign of the creature. He kept up his rigorous exercises for almost three months, then let them tail off; after all, he reasoned, he was just going to shoot the damned thing, not wrestle with it.

The first six months in space were uneventful. The next twenty were even worse. Vostuvian was quite content to go weeks on end without saying a word, and Lane was damned if he was going to be the first one to break the silence. He had never begged for anything in his life, and he sure as hell wasn't going to beg an alien he had grown to hate to talk to him.

So time continued to drag. Even the Mufti became irritable, and Lane finally put it into Deepsleep. When their thirtieth month in dust cloud came and went with no noticeable change, he went back to his exercise routine, and took regular stints outside the *Deathmaker*, letting the ship tow him via a lifeline.

He stopped wondering where the creature was hiding and started to wonder if it was dead. He wanted to make radio contact with other ships or ports and find out if there had been any recent sightings, but the knowledge that he must surely have a price on his head by this time always prevented him from doing so. So he sat, and watched, and waited.

When the *Deathmaker* was thirty-three months out from Belore a fast-moving object showed up on Lane's instrument panel, but a moment later the sensors confirmed that it was merely an old cargo ship on a milk run. Still, the incident seemed to reawaken the predator in him, and he spent another month glued to his instrument panel before he became convinced that one solitary sighting didn't necessarily presage any others.

They were thirty-eight long, boring, silent months out from Belore when it finally happened. Lane was exercising on the outside of the ship, walking up and down the length of the hull with heavy, magnetic boots, flicking the magnets on and off with each step, when he heard Vostuvian's calm, unhurried voice in his earphone.

"I think you had better come in, Lane."

"Something malfunctioning?" asked Lane.

"No."

"Is it the Mufti?" he asked, walking laboriously to the nearest airlock.

"No," said Vostuvian. "I think I have spotted the *straigor*."

"The what?"

"The Dreamwish Beast."

Lane was inside in another three minutes, and bending over the instrument panel thirty seconds after that.

"It's the creature, all right!" he said, unfastening his space suit and throwing it on the floor in a heap.

"About half a million miles, I should estimate," said Vostuvian.

Lane brought the ship to a halt, then began edging forward. If the creature really could sense the presence of the diluter, he wanted to get as close as he could before it knew he was there. The *Deathmaker* got to within two hundred thousand miles, and just as Lane was releasing the various safety mechanisms from the diluter, the creature took off like a bat out of hell.

The *Deathmaker* jumped forward in pursuit. It had lost another fifty thousand miles before Lane could react, but now, as both creature and ship approached light speeds, the interval remained constant.

"It's veering away from the dust cloud," remarked Vostuvian tonelessly.

"It knows I mean business this time," said Lane, his eyes and hands never leaving the instrument panels. "What did you say the maximum effective range of this thing is?"

"About seventy thousand miles," said the Dorne.

"That's for killing, right?"

"I do not understand you, Lane," said Vostuvian.

"If I can maneuver to within, say, one hundred and twenty thousand miles, will the diluter be able to wing it?"

"Wing it?"

"Wound it," said Lane. "Slow it down."

"I doubt it," said Vostuvian. "And, while seventy thousand miles is the maximum range, I feel you would be far wiser to hold your fire until you are less than thirty thousand miles away."

"Both those problems are going to be academic until it

starts running out of juice," said Lane. "We're going damned near maximum right now, and I'd be surprised if we're gaining much more than ten yards a minute."

The creature had indeed left the dust cloud and was now racing in a straight, true line toward the galactic rim, some tens of thousands of light-years distant. And running just as straight and just as true was the *Deathmaker*.

Three days into the chase Lane, despite all his efforts and amphetamines, fell asleep at the panel, and Vostuvian worked the controls for the next eleven hours. When Lane awoke there had been no appreciable change in the positions of the ship and the quarry.

Nor was there any change for the next month. Once or twice Lane thought he had lost it, for his ship's sensing devices were far less efficient at light speeds, but the creature remained on course, and sooner or later Lane was always able to get a reading on it.

They were approaching the Outer Frontier now and still there had been no letup in the creature's speed. Lane began to seriously wonder if it ever required rest. He put the question to Vostuvian.

"Who can say?" replied the Dorne. "When my people waged war on them, they made no effort to escape, so I have no data upon which to base a conclusion."

"In other words, it is conceivable to you that we may chase this thing the rest of our lives and never get appreciably closer to it."

"It is a possibility," said the Dorne. "However, any life form, no matter how unique in composition, must have limits of energy expenditure which cannot be transgressed."

"True," said Lane. "But since this creature has been around for eons, there's no reason to assume that those limits will occur in our lifetimes, is there?"

"No," said Vostuvian emotionlessly.

"There used to be a saying about a prophet named Mohammed and a mountain," said Lane. "I won't quote it to you, since you probably wouldn't understand or appreciate it, but I think I'm going to apply its principle."

With that, he pressed the firing mechanism on the vibrator and aimed it in the direction of the fleeing creature. For ten minutes there was no reaction; then slowly, almost imperceptibly, it began to slow down. Lane slowed the *Deathmaker* down as well, keeping a quarter-million-mile distance between them.

Within an hour both the creature and the ship were at rest, and Lane began firing the vibrator at twenty-second intervals.

And then, carefully and tentatively, the creature began approaching the ship. When it got to within one hundred fifty thousand miles Lane felt a wave of eagerness spread over him, and realized, with a sense of mortification and shame, that the creature was still too far away for it to be any emotion other than his own.

Now it was within one hundred thousand miles, and suddenly it paused, throbbing wildly.

"What's the matter with it?" asked Lane.

"Indecision, I should suspect," said Vostuvian. "It knows who you are now, but it also senses the entropy weapon."

It remained, motionless and pulsating, for another hour, and Lane didn't dare move the *Deathmaker* up to meet it. Once again he removed the safety devices from the diluter, and waited.

Finally the creature began inching forward again, slowly and hesitantly. When it got within eighty thousand miles it stopped.

"Now what?" asked Vostuvian. It was the first curiosity he had displayed since learning how to pilot the ship.

"Now we wait," said Lane. "It seems to know the limits of the diluter, so it's probably going to take some time to muster up enough courage to come any closer."

It took almost a full Standard day, but finally the creature began approaching them again. Now it was within maximum range, now sixty thousand miles, now forty-five.

Suddenly Lane began shaking in earnest, and he knew that he was *en rapport* with the creature again. He locked the diluter's sights onto it and waited.

"Shoot now!" rasped Vostuvian, and Lane saw that his companion was trembling even more than he was.

"Not yet," said Lane. "I've got to be sure this time."

"Now!" screamed Vostuvian.

"Shut up!" snapped Lane.

"It's within range!" shouted Vostuvian. "What are you waiting for?"

The creature was within twenty-five thousand miles now. It was approaching the ship more gingerly, but still approaching.

Lane could feel it, feel fear and apprehension and excitement and lust and longing. And something else he had never before felt.

Loneliness.

Vostuvian was jabbering insanely now, and suddenly he lunged for the diluter's firing mechanism. Lane shoved him away.

"Kill it!" shrieked the Dorne.

Lane rose from his chair and stood between Vostuvian and the diluter.

"Keep away from this weapon or the creature's not the only thing I'm going to kill," he said, trying to control his voice.

The creature was close enough to be seen on the main viewing screen now, and Lane turned to look at it. It was throbbing gently, its colors changing back and forth subtly, as it continued its inexorable approach.

Lane placed his hand on the firing mechanism, and now, along with the fear and the lust and the loneliness, came yet another feeling: trust.

Lane tried to fire the weapon, tried with every ounce of willpower he possessed—and found that he couldn't. His hand moved, almost independently of his brain, along the master control panel until it came to the vibrator's firing mechanism.

In the tiny section of his mind that was clear and rational, he computed how much time it would take to recover from using the vibrator and still get off a shot on the diluter. Fifteen seconds, possibly twenty. Could the creature get away that quickly? He didn't know, but he doubted it.

And, cursing his weakness, he fired the vibrator.

Vostuvian was hurled back against the far wall of the cabin, but Lane remained on his feet, rigid and unblinking. He let wave after wave of the creature's sensations and emotions cascade over him, suffusing him in a warm, pulsating, satiated glow.

Then, as the creature began retreating, he moved his hand back to the diluter. It was forty thousand miles away now, and moving leisurely. All he had to do was press the firing mechanism and it would be dead.

But he wanted to be certain.

He lined it up again, cleared his previous order to his tracking and locking mechanisms and gave it to them again, checked his panel to make sure the creature hadn't applied any evasive actions.

And then, at one hundred twelve thousand miles, he fired the diluter.

And missed.

CHAPTER
20

It was many minutes before Lane came to a full realization of what he had done, and many hours before Vostuvian was completely conscious.

"It's changed directions," said Lane, when he saw that the Dorne could understand him. "It's heading toward the core."

"I knew it," muttered Vostuvian. "I knew you wouldn't kill it."

"I fired the diluter," said Lane. "It was out of range."

"Out of range?" repeated Vostuvian. His voice was barely audible now, probably as a result of his earlier yelling. "Lane, it was within twenty thousand miles."

"You broke my concentration," said Lane. "I had it beaten, and then you started going for the diluter. Up until that instant I was in control."

"You were never in control," said Vostuvian, once again inscrutable and unemotional.

"I was!" snapped Lane. "I was fighting it off! I was ready to fire when it got closer, and then you messed everything up."

"Not so, Lane," said the Dorne. "Don't you know yet that you can't destroy it by yourself?"

"I'm not convinced that I can destroy it with you on board," said Lane. "Now just shut up and leave me alone."

He checked his panel. The creature was almost six hundred thousand miles ahead of them, and once again going at light speeds. After another hour he had Vostuvian take over the controls while he went back to the galley for something to eat.

He stared at his storeroom of concentrates, decided he wasn't hungry after all, and sat at the mess table, staring unblinking at a bulkhead.

Just how much of what he had said to the Dorne was true, and how much was a rationalization? He didn't want to come to grips with it, but he had to. He had to know what he would do the next time he got the creature in his sights, had to know which weapon he would use.

And, as he thought about it, his rage transferred itself from Vostuvian to the creature. It was the creature that had warped his mind and his judgment and his senses, not Vostuvian. It was the creature that made him fire the vibrator rather than the diluter, that made him wait too long to finally bring the entropy weapon into play, that had turned him into an obscene *thing* with unthinkable longings. Vostuvian didn't inhabit his nightmares and his daydreams and his fantasies; the creature did.

He'd had it within his grasp and let it get away. But he'd taken everything it had to give, and missed it only by a matter of seconds. Now he knew what it could and couldn't do to him, what he could and couldn't do to it. The battle lines were drawn. Next time he would be ready for it, next time there would be no hesitation, next time he'd take a chance on winging it if he had to.

Next time . . .

But the next time didn't materialize as soon as Lane had hoped it would. Their mad flight continued for days that stretched into weeks that stretched into months, back toward the galactic Greenwich. The Outer Frontier was behind them, and soon they passed through the Democracy as well, and then they were at the Inner Frontier. Man hadn't built his empire from the galactic core outward, but from Earth and Deluros VIII and half a dozen other major worlds in huge, ever-widening circles. And, while he hadn't expanded anywhere near the rim yet, he also hadn't gone much farther toward the geocentric core than Northpoint and a few hundred other worlds on the periphery of human civilization.

On and on they raced, past millions of unexplored worlds, and finally into an area that was not only unexplored but uncharted.

"If it doesn't slow down one of these days," said Lane as he tried, for perhaps the thousandth time, to entice the creature by firing his vibrator at regular intervals, "I'm going to shoot the damned diluter after it anyway. Maybe we'll get lucky."

"The greatest stroke of luck in such a case would be not to outrun the beam and be destroyed ourselves," said Vostuvian.

Lane grunted an answer that was neither positive nor negative nor complimentary, and turned his attention back to the board.

And then, so unexpectedly that it made both of them jump, the *Deathmaker* received a radio signal, its first in years.

"Repeating: Mayday," said a thin but recognizably human voice which was barely discernible due to excessive static. "Repeating: Mayday. Condition urgent."

Lane reached over and switched on his transmitter.

"This is the *Deathmaker*, Nicobar Lane commanding, forty-five months out of Belore."

"Thank God!" said the voice. "This is Jonas Stonemason, captain of the *Rachel*. All our power is gone, and we have at most another two days of air and water remaining."

"What the hell are you doing out here?" said Lane.

"This is a colony ship," said Stonemason. "I was searching for an agricultural world on the Inner Frontier when all my power went dead. We were going at about fifty percent light speed when it happened, and our inertia has carried us here. We only just got the radio working four days ago. Will you help us?''

"I can't," said Lane. "This ship has urgent business elsewhere."

"Damn it, man!" snapped Stonemason. "I have more than six hundred women and children on board! We've homed in on your signal, and estimate our paths will cross within half a million miles in about five hours."

Lane switched off the radio and checked his instrument panel. The creature was still racing its accustomed margin ahead of them, and he knew that if he even slowed down, let alone effected a rescue operation, the hunt would be over, perhaps forever.

He opened communications again.

"*Rachel?* This is the *Deathmaker*. I have a small ship, too small to aid you in any way. I will pass word of your situation and give your coordinates and speed to any and all ships I encounter."

"Damn you, Lane!" bellowed Stonemason. "You're condemning more than a thousand colonists to die!"

"It can't be helped," said Lane. "You'll have to believe me when I tell you that I regret it deeply, and would aid you if it were at all possible."

"There's nothing more important than saving the lives of your fellow men!" said Stonemaston. "I beg of you, Lane: please give us your help."

"I can't," said Lane, trying not to think about a thousand bodies with black, bloated tongues and huge popping eyes.

He thought he detected the sound of a scuffle, and then a feminine voice, half sobbing and half screaming, came on.

"Mr. Lane, I speak not only for myself and my two daughters, but for the whole ship. What is more important than performing an act of mercy?''

''You wouldn't understand. Believe me, I'd help you if I could.''

''Mr. Lane, I beg of you, please—''

Lane reached over to the radio and broke off communication.

Then, turning the controls over to Vostuvian, he walked to his hammock and lay down, hands behind his head. He should have helped the *Rachel*; or, failing that, he should at least have felt guilty. But he didn't. All he felt was eagerness to come to grips with the creature once again.

And suddenly, as he thought of all those doomed colonists, and the members of the Roanoke Colony, and the miners on Bastion, and the Mariner, and the seemingly endless years in space, and the entropy weapon that was never fired until too late, he knew the creature's name. Not Dreamwish Beast, or Sunlighter, or *straigor*, or Starduster, or Deathdealer, or any of the other labels that had been given it, but its true name, the only name that could ever describe it.

And in that instant, Nicobar Lane rededicated himself to the slaying of the Soul Eater.

CHAPTER
21

The chase continued unabated for another fifty-three days. The ship's fuel and food supplies were holding up well, but Lane estimated that they'd be out of water in another month or so; and, since he had no idea how soon he would be able to kill the Soul Eater, he set Vostuvian to the task of jury-rigging a recycling system.

And then, fifty-four days after leaving the *Rachel* to flounder and die in the trackless wastes of space, they came to the galactic core.

And found the granddaddy of all black holes.

It had been postulated for centuries that every spiral galaxy had an enormous black hole at its center. Now this one stretched before Lane, some three hundred thirty million miles in diameter, almost as large as the orbit of Mars. He couldn't see it, of course; by its very nature it absorbed all light and reflected none. But the *Deathmaker's* instrument panel picked up its gravitational field and recorded the limits of its event horizon.

"Get ready," Lane said, taking over manual control of the ship. "It's got to change directions any minute now."

But the Soul Eater, approaching the hole at an angle, veered neither right nor left, neither up nor down.

"I've seen it pull this stunt before," said Lane. "It'll run right up to the hole and shear off at the last second.

"It will have to do so soon, Lane," said Vostuvian. "Another three minutes and it will be inside the hole."

Lane released the diluter's safety devices and tried to lock onto the Soul Eater, but the creature was too far away.

"We'd better slow down, Lane," said the Dorne, "or we will be unable to escape the hole's gravitational field."

"Uh-uh," said Lane. "First, a hole that big doesn't have as much of a field at the event horizon as a smaller one. And second, I'm not letting the Soul Eater get away this time."

"You're not thinking clearly," said Vostuvian. "Its field will be immense. It has already absorbed most of the stars from the core."

"You've been planetbound too long," said Lane, never taking his eyes from the instrument panel. "The event horizon doesn't cause the field; the singularity—the point that all the matter is drawn to—does. And the event horizon of a hole like this is much farther from the singularity than it would be on a small hole. We're going straight ahead."

The Dorne made no answer, and the chase went on. Far ahead of them the Soul Eater raced headlong for the hole, and even Lane wondered how much longer it could wait before veering away from the yawning black pit.

"It's going to go into the hole!" said Vostuvian. "Bank away from it now, Lane, before it's too late."

Lane made no answer, and suddenly the Dorne pushed him away and reached for the control panel.

"Get away, Vostuvian," said Lane. "I'm only going to tell you once."

The Dorne paid no attention to him, and Lane drew his screecher and fired it. Vostuvian screamed, went absolutely rigid, and then collapsed in a lifeless heap on the deck.

Lane kicked the body out of the way and ran to the panel, making sure that the ship was still matching speed and direction with the Soul Eater. It was, and he turned a portion of his attention to the diluter. If he guessed which direction the creature would veer, he'd be able to get a shot off; if not, he'd lose another seven hundred thousand miles before he got the ship squared away.

And then his jaw fell open as he realized that Vostuvian had been right. The Soul Eater had no intention of veering away from the black hole; it was too late now, even if it wanted to. In another five seconds it would disappear beyond the event horizon, swallowed by an enormous negation that had crushed cosmic debris, planets, even giant stars, down to a dimensionless point.

Lane had bare seconds to make a decision, and realized that it had been made long before. With a bellowing curse, he directed the *Deathmaker* into the yawning chasm of nothingness that had just clutched the Soul Eater to its unknown and unknowable bosom.

CHAPTER
22

Lane expected to be stretched almost to infinity and crushed to death at the same instant.

Neither happened.

Later, when he realized that he was going to live, he spent a considerable amount of time trying to figure out what had occurred, but never quite understood it.

He knew everything in the universe rotated—including, especially, collapsing stars. Neutron stars, which hadn't been quite massive enough to collapse beyond that stage to become black holes, rotated on their axes at a rate of once a second or even faster. What Lane didn't know—and wouldn't have cared about had he known—was that when a black hole begins forming, the collapsing star's rotation rate speeds up almost beyond computation. By so doing, it distorts the black hole to such a degree that it forms not one, but two event horizons.

Had the *Deathmaker* gone beyond both event horizons, everything Lane had expected would have occurred. His feet, being almost two meters nearer the singularity, would have been drawn down toward that awesome point at a faster rate than his head. He would have been literally pulled apart, though the excessive gravitational field would have killed him long before that happened.

But the *Deathmaker* did not pierce both event horizons. It followed the path of the Soul Eater *between* the two horizons, and was flung completely out of its own time and space by the unimaginable power of that rotating field.

It was not the mystical hyperspace or superspace imagined by fanciful writers, nor the wormholes in the fabric of space postulated by speculative scientists, nor even the bending and curving of space hidden in Einstein's calculations. Nor was it a timewarp or spacewarp, though those words perhaps best describe the effect. It was, plainly and simply, the momentary negation of all time and all space, the only such negation possible under the laws that govern the universe.

Lane experienced no dizziness, no nausea, no sense of disorientation. He knew who he was, and thought he knew where he was, at all times. None of his instruments worked, his clocks started doing crazy things, and his viewing screens made absolutely no sense.

And, suddenly, after an indeterminate and undeterminable passage of time, he was—elsewhere.

The *Deathmaker*'s systems began working again, and he tried to determine exactly where his ship had been hurled. None of his standard galactic reference points were visible, and he was unable even to guess where he was.

Then he looked out through his viewing screen, and realized that he didn't even know *when* he was.

He was in some universe, but whether it was his own or not he couldn't tell, nor did he ever learn. But whatever universe it was, it was in its infancy. Huge as it was—and, by their very definition, all universes are huge—it was more compact than the one he had known. There were precious few stars as such, but in their place were millions upon millions of superstars, each the size of a red or blue giant, but burning with an intensity that almost blinded him even from thousands of parsecs away. They hung against the velvet background of space like huge sparkling jewels, shooting off their unbelievably bright substance in billion-mile streams and jets, spinning so rapidly that he could almost see the minute variations in their intensity.

He knew then that they were quasars, and concluded that they were embryonic galaxies—unless this was a contracting old age rather than an expanding infancy, in which case they were the end result of galactic lives rather than the proud beginnings. He leaned toward his first conclusion, but he gave the matter very little thought, for a quarter of a million miles away from him floated the Soul Eater.

The creature was his only reference point in a strange universe, the only fixed and known quantity in a time and space that would be forever alien to him. It was even possible that they were the only two living things in the whole of this Creation.

And one of them would have to die.

With a snarl he plunged the *Deathmaker* forward. The Soul Eater seemed unaware of his presence until he had pulled to within seventy-five thousand miles of it, and then it jumped ahead. He followed it for an hour, unable to close the gap between them. His hand inched over to the diluter. He knew he had to fire it before the creature eluded him and left him stranded here, lost and alone.

He pressed the firing mechanism.

Instantly, inside his head, he heard, or felt, or sensed, an inhuman howl of anguish. The Soul Eater wobbled crazily and changed directions continuously, while a portion of it turned a bright blue, then a dull gray, and finally vanished. A few moments later it had regained its spherical shape, though smaller now, and began evasive maneuvering at a somewhat diminished speed.

The sensation of pain was no longer as sharp as it had been, and Lane was able to begin manipulating the ship's control panel. And then, added to the physical pain, was a feeling of uncomprehending *hurt*. Not bitter, not angry, not resentful, but puzzled, as a puppy feels toward the child who kicks it.

Lane couldn't stand any more of the emotional agony, and he slowed the *Deathmaker* until the creature was out of sending range. Then it began moving in a straight line, and, adjusting the ship's speed to that of the Soul Eater, Lane followed it at a distance of two hundred thousand miles.

He put the ship on automatic control and, for the first time, surveyed the interior of the pilot's cabin. Vostuvian's corpse lay at an awkward angle, its blind eyes staring at him in reproach while its lips grimaced horribly. Lane dragged the body to an airlock and jettisoned it—and then, suddenly panic-stricken, he raced to the Deepsleep chambers.

The Mufti was dead, as he had known it would be, its metabolism halted when the ship's systems were shut down during the trip through the black hole.

He lifted the little animal gingerly out of its chamber and cradled it in his arms, stroking it gently and methodically. Numb and miserable, he walked back to the pilot's cabin, still carrying it, and sat down, holding it so tightly that it would have been screaming in pain had it been alive.

Finally, when the animal's body started to stiffen, he gently carried it to the airlock, and a moment later the Lord High Mufti was jettisoned into space. Space could be kind to a body, or grotesquely capricious. Lane had seen what happened to a man whose spacesuit was ripped open while he was still alive, and it wasn't a pretty sight. On the other hand, space would treat his little pet benevolently, preserving its body and features as it floated there for all eternity, and for that Lane was glad.

Then he turned his attention back to the Soul Eater.

It was all he had left. Vostuvian was dead, the Mufti was dead, the universe he had known was as good as dead. It was just the two of them now. Nothing else, no one else mattered, or even existed.

He was pretty sure he could kill it at will. It was crippled, and his instruments showed that it was now only about five miles in diameter.

But he couldn't rid his mind and memory of its reaction when he had wounded it. It had trusted him, just as the Mufti had, and he didn't feel like killing two trusting creatures in a single day. Tomorrow would be soon enough.

But the next day the Soul Eater had regained some of its strength and increased its speed. Also, whether from disorientation or panic, it began shifting directions again, and Lane had no choice but to follow it.

They remained thus for almost a week, and suddenly a new element entered into Lane's considerations: he had spent more fuel matching the creature's maneuvering during the past six days than he had spent chasing it all the way up to the black hole. If he continued using fuel at this rate, his tanks would be empty in another ten days.

The Soul Eater continued to change directions every few hours for the next six days, and now Lane knew beyond any shadow of a doubt that if he didn't kill it soon he would never be able to.

And then the Soul Eater began to slow down. Possibly it had finally expended its seemingly endless supply of energy, possibly it was feeling the aftereffects of the diluter, possibly it was taunting him. But whatever the reason, he soon pulled to within one hundred thousand miles, then eighty, then forty, and then both the creature and its pursuer came to a stop, twelve thousand miles apart.

Suddenly Lane realized that he didn't feel the accompanying tension that always came with the Soul Eater's presence. Instead he felt old, tired, weary, with a horrible, aching, overwhelming loneliness.

The Soul Eater had given up. It was ready to die, tired of running away, unable to understand how something it trusted could hurt it so badly. It waved no white flag, requested no peace conference.

It had surrendered unconditionally.

Lane placed his hand on the diluter's firing mechanism—and stopped.

He gazed at the creature through his viewing screen, and it looked old and beaten. Its color was dull and unchanging, its body no longer pulsated and throbbed with energy, its shape remained constant.

He tried to analyze the Soul Eater's emotions. There was no anger, no hatred, no outrage against destiny; there was just resignation, and a desire to get the inevitable over with as quickly as possible.

This was the moment Lane had lived for for more years than he could remember, the moment he had longed for and killed for and robbed for and lied for. It was his ultimate triumph, the victory for which he had traded his career and his wealth and his youth. He removed his hand from the diluter. This was a moment to be savored for as long as possible. The creature was beaten and humbled; it would make no attempt to escape. He could pause for awhile to enjoy the taste of victory.

It tasted bitter.

He thought of Tchaka's parting question, and found that he still couldn't answer it. What *would* he do after he fired the diluter?

He was a hunter. He needed his quarry every bit as much as this particular quarry needed him. Even if he died a week from now, it would be the loneliest, emptiest, most meaningless week of his life.

And then he realized that Tchaka's question had barely scratched the surface. He no longer drank, he had no use for drugs, women didn't interest him, and he knew that, having experienced the Soul Eater, nothing less than that ever could please him again. He had no family, no friends, only a handful of acquaintances. His money was almost gone, his office building sold, his profession a distant memory. All he had, all that remained, was the defeated beast hovering near the *Deathmaker*.

Did he hate it for what it had done to his life?

Yes.

But he knew, with a certainty that admitted of no argument, that he needed it even more than he hated it.

"Oh, hell," he said softly. Then carefully, almost tenderly, he aimed the vibrator at the very center of the Soul Eater and pressed the firing mechanism.

And, instead of the usual physical and mental thunderbolt, he felt a gentle emotional tendril reach out and encompass him, flowing through every inch, every molecule, every atom of his body and mind. It lingered lovingly, gratefully, and then withdrew.

Lane spent a few minutes trying to analyze what the creature had felt and his reaction to it. When he had finally sorted out his emotions, and, strangely, found them unrepugnant, the creature reached out to him again.

And this time there was neither pain nor loneliness.

CHAPTER
23

They stayed there for a long time, the hunter and the hunted.

Then one day the Soul Eater began moving away very slowly, and Lane, puzzled, followed it. It soon increased its speed, but Lane held the *Deathmaker* at a constant velocity, very conscious of his diminishing fuel supply. After a few minutes the creature adjusted its pace to that of the ship.

And at last they came to a black hole, almost as large as the one through which they had entered this time and space. There was no swirling vortex of gas or debris, for the hole had assimilated all such matter long ago. There was, instead, an almost tangible absence of anything but the hole itself.

The Soul Eater made three approaches before it finally came in at the exact angle that suited it, and Lane had no choice but to match it, move for move. Then they were between the event horizons.

Once again Lane expected to experience some physical reaction, and once again he felt nothing at all. He looked ahead, and could see the Soul Eater far in front of him; then he tried to look back, and found that he could see absolutely nothing of the universe he was leaving.

He had no idea how long he spent inside the black hole,

or how far he had traveled, for time and distance had no meaning there, but eventually the *Deathmaker* was hurled into another universe.

His universe.

He checked his stellar reference points, fed them into the computer, and found that he was halfway between the galactic core and the Inner Frontier. The Soul Eater had waited for the ship, and now hovered a few hundred miles away, undulating in little waves.

He went over the ship's systems, determined that they were still in good working order, and decided that fuel and water were his first concerns. He laid in a course for Rabot VI, the nearest frontier world which he knew to have fueling facilities. He soon reached light speed and then let the ship's inertia carry it along, while the Soul Eater raced beside it.

Finally, many weeks later, he began decelerating as he approached Rabot VI. The creature realized that he was going to land and flashed him, in quick succession, feelings of puzzlement, hurt, misery, and panic. He tried to reassure it, to assuage its fears, but he didn't know how. Then, as he put the *Deathmaker* into orbit prior to receiving his landing coordinates and clearance, the creature's terror got the better of it and it raced off in the opposite direction.

He filled his fuel and water tanks up, laid in still more food, and tried without success to learn if the *Rachel* had been found yet. Finally, when everything was in order, the *Deathmaker* took off for the last time.

The Soul Eater was waiting for him out beyond Rabot, as he had known it would be. Then, content and serene, they matched velocities and continued their endless voyage through the trackless void, which seemed somehow to have become a little smaller and a little less frightening.

EPILOGUE

Time passed.

Years came and went, as years do. The Democracy was experiencing one final burst of strength and solidity before its final dissolution. The credit was stable again, but only momentarily. Devilowls had been added to the ever-growing list of extinct species. The cure for eplasia was not as comprehensive as originally believed, and the disease still lingered on. And, as always, the frontier worlds gave all such developments little notice and less thought.

Tchaka's was crowded.

Rubbing shoulders at every table were the hunters, the explorers, the adventurers, the misfits who had elected to come out to the frontier. At the back of the room was a crew of Dabihs, seeking employment as skinners on a hunting expedition. By the door were four black marketeers, each trying to outwit and outbluff the others. Standing where the light would show him off to best advantage was a brilliantly clad and bejeweled miner who had just hit it rich. Two of Tchaka's whores leaned against one end of the long, polished bar, taking their equivalent of a coffee break.

Tchaka himself was tending the bar. He was a few pounds heavier, his face was a little more lined, the knuckles of his right hand were still swollen from a brawl the previous week, but he was as imposing and vigorous a figure as ever. His artificial eye flashed and sparkled brilliantly, and the little lizard in his earlobe represented his thirty-seventh generation of living jewelry.

Three young men, bearded and mustached in an attempt to belie their ages, their hats affixed at just the proper jaunty angles, their boots a little too new and too clean, sat at a table near the bar. They had been swapping their limited store of tall tales, and a mild argument had ensued.

"Ask Tchaka," said one of them. "He'll know."

"Might as well," agreed another. "Hey, Tchaka, can you give us a little help?"

"Blonde or redhead?" Tchaka grinned. "I'm always willing to help a paying customer."

"Later," said the young man. "We need a little information first."

"Ask away," said Tchaka, leaning across the bar to pinch one of his whores as she strutted past.

"My companions here," said the young man, with just the proper note of condescension in his voice, "seem to think there's something to the new *Flying Dutchman* legend."

"I don't even know the old one," said Tchaka.

"The original one concerned a captain who had to sail Earth's oceans for all eternity until the curse was lifted by the love of a woman. But now there's supposed to be some incredibly ancient man way out past the frontier, who's doomed to keep chasing someone or something that no one else has ever seen."

"They say his ship never lands," said another of the men, "and that he races away whenever anyone approaches him."

"And you're asking my opinion?" said Tchaka.

"Yes. What do you think?"

"I like the first version better," said Tchaka with a smile that nobody understood.

"That's not what I mean," said the young man. "What about the story? Do you know if it's true or not?"

A grizzled old miner who had been listening intently sidled over to them. "Just a fable dreamed up by some feeble-minded spacehand to pass the time of day," he said. "You might just as well believe in"—he searched for the right example—"oh, in the Dreamwish Beast."

The three sophisticated young men all laughed at that. A moment later Tchaka joined them, and as he threw back his head his golden teeth glowed like tiny yellow stars in the vast cavern of his mouth.

Mike Resnick was born and raised in the Chicago area. He attended the University of Chicago, where he met his wife, Carol, ''and majored in absenteeism.'' They were married in 1961, and their daughter, Laura, an award-winning writer herself, was born a year later.

Mike and Carol bred and exhibited collies with enormous success during the 1960s and 1970s, and they purchased the country's second-largest boarding and grooming kennel, which they still own and operate in Cincinnati.

Mike wrote in a number of other fields prior to 1981, when he began concentrating almost exclusively on his first love, science-fiction. Since that time he has produced such well-received novels as the bestselling *Santiago*, the Nebula-nominated *Ivory*, *Soothsayer*, *Oracle*, *Stalking the Unicorn*, and of course *Adventures*, the book that brought Lucifer Jones to the world.

He was never very interested in short fiction until the mid-1980s, when he began turning it out in quantity. The downstate returns aren't all in yet, but when last we looked he had won Hugo awards for ''Kirinyaga'' and ''The Manamouki,'' and had also been nominated for a number of other brilliant stories.

Mike and Carol spend a month in Africa every year, and they are also much in demand on the science-fiction convention circuit.

AN EXCERPT FROM

Lucifer Jones

BY
MIKE
RESNICK

A NOVEMBER 1992
QUESTAR RELEASE

The
Master
Detective

They say that there are a lot of differences between Hong Kong and some of the African cities I recently left behind. Different people, different cultures, different buildings, even different food.

Of course, there are a lot of similarities, too. Same lack of consideration for those who are bold enough to tinker with the laws of statistical probability. Same steel bars in the local jail. Same concrete walls and floors. Same uncomfortable cots. Same awful food.

Truth to tell, I'd had a lot more time to consider the similarities than the differences. I'd gotten right off the boat from Portuguese East Africa, checked into the Luk Kwok Hotel (which thoughtfully rented its rooms by the hour, the night, or the week), spent the next hour in a local restaurant trying to down a bowl of soup with a pair of chopsticks, and then, realizing that my funds needed replenishing, I got involved in a friendly little game of chance involving two cubes of ivory with spots painted on them. It was when a third cube slipped out of my sleeve that I was invited to inspect the premises of the local jail.

That was five days ago, and I had spent the intervening time alternately trying not to mind the smell of dead fish, which is what all of Hong Kong smelled like back in 1926, and gaining some comfort by reading my well-worn copy of the Good Book, which I ain't never without.

The girl who brought my grub to me was a charming little thing named Mei Sung. She was right impressed to be serving a man of the cloth, which I was back in those days, and I converted the bejabbers out of her three or four times a day, which made my incarceration in durance vile a mite easier to take.

As time crawled by I got to know my fellow inmates. There was a Turkish dentist who had gassed a British officer to death in what he assured me was an accident and would certainly have been construed as such by the courts if he hadn't appropriated the officer's wallet and wristwatch before reporting the poor fellow's untimely demise. There was a young Brazilian student who sweated up a storm and kept screaming things about anarchy and tyrants and such and keeping everyone awake. There were two Chinamen dressed all in black, who kept glaring at me every time I finished converting Mei Sung. There was a Frenchman who kept saying he was glad he had killed the chef, and that anyone who ruined *sole amandine* that badly deserved to die.

And there was me, the Right Reverend Honorable Doctor Lucifer Jones, out of Moline, Illinois, by way of the Dark Continent, where I'd done my best to illuminate the dark, dreary lives of the godless black heathen despite certain minor disagreements with the constabularies of fourteen countries, which culminated in my being asked to establish the Tabernacle of Saint Luke on some other land mass. But I already wrote that story, and I ain't going to go into it again, since anyone who's read it knows that I'm a righteous and God-fearing man who was just misunderstood.

On the fifth day of the thirty that I was to serve, they gave me a roommate, a well-dressed Australian with expensive-looking rings on all his fingers. His name was Rupert Cornwall, and he explained that he had come to Hong Kong because Australia was a pretty empty country and he liked crowds.

"And what do you do for a living, Brother Rupert?" I asked him, by way of being polite.

"I'm an entrepreneur," he said. "I put opportunists together with opportunities, and take a little percentage for my trouble."

"I didn't know being an entrepreneur was a criminal offense in Hong Kong," I said.

"I was arrested by mistake," he answered. "You, too?"

"Absolutely," he said. "I expect to be out of here within the hour. And what about yourself? You look like a man of God with that turned-around collar of yours."

"You hit the nail right on the head, Brother Rupert. That's what I am: a man of God, here to bring comfort and spiritual uplifting to the heathen."

"What religion do you belong to?" he asked.

"One me and the Lord worked out betwixt ourselves one Sunday afternoon back in Illinois," I said. "Hell, the way I see it, as long as we're upright and holy and got a poorbox, what's the difference?"

He broke out into a great big smile. "I *like* you, Doctor Jones," he said. "Where's your church located?"

"Well, I ain't quite got around to building my tabernacle yet, Brother Rupert . . . but I'm taking donations for it, if the spirit's come upon you and you're so inclined."

"I don't have any money with me," he answered. "But look me up after we're both out of here, and I might have some work for you."

"Work wasn't exactly what I had in mind," I said distastefully.

"When you hear what I have to offer, you might change your mind," he said.

"Yeah?"

He nodded. "I could use a man of the cloth in my operation. I think we could enter into a mutually profitable relationship."

"You don't say?" I replied. "Well, I suppose I could always take a brief fling at the entrepreneur business before I erect my tabernacle, God being the patient and understanding soul that He is."

He reached into his vest pocket and handed me his card. "That's my business address. Remember to call on me."

Well, I could tell we were hitting it off right fine and I was going to ask him more about our pending partnership, but just then a guard came by and unlocked the door.

"They made your bail again, Rupert," he said in a bored voice.

"Was there ever any doubt?" asked Rupert smugly.

"You get arrested by mistake a lot?" I asked as he was leaving.

"Almost daily," he said. "Personally, I think they're just jealous of my success."

Then he was gone, and I was left with my thoughts until Mei Sung came by for another conversion, which left me so exhausted that I thought I might grab a quick forty winks. I had snored my way through about twenty of 'em when the door opened again, and the guard gestured me to follow him.

"Did somebody make my bail, too?" I asked, thinking of Rupert Cornwall. He just chuckled and kept leading me down one corridor after another until we finally came to a little cubbyhole, which was filled with a desk, two chairs, and a pudgy Chinaman with a natty little mustache and goatee. He was dressed in a white linen suit, and hadn't bothered to take his Panama hat off even though we were inside.

"Sit, please," he said, smiling at me.

I sat myself down in the empty chair while he nodded at the guard, who left the room.

"You are Mr. Jones?" said the Chinaman.

"Doctor Lucifer Jones at your service," I said.

"That what we must talk about," he said in pidgin English.

"About whether I'm Lucifer Jones?" I asked, puzzled.

"About whether you are at my service," he said. "Because if not, then you go back to cell for twenty-five more days."

"Are you the guy who made my bail?" I asked.

"No one make your bail," he said. "Please sit back and relax, Doctor Jones. I am Inspector Willie Wong of Hong Kong Police Force. Perhaps you have heard of me?"

"Can't say that I have, Brother Wong," I answered. He looked right disappointed at that.

"Why are you wasting your time with me, anyway?" I continued. "You ought to be trying to find the ungodly sinner that stuck that extra die up my sleeve."

"That no concern of mine," he said, holding up a hand. "But am prepared to make deal, Doctor Jones. You help me, I help you."

"Yeah?"

He nodded. "Man in your cell named Rupert Cornwall."

"What about him?"

"Rupert Cornwall biggest gangster in Hong Kong."

"Then why did you let him go?"

"Beauty is in eye of beholder," said Wong.

"I beg your pardon?"

"Old Chinese proverb. Perhaps it not translate very well." He paused. "Let Rupert Cornwall go for lack of evidence."

"What has all this got to do with me?" I asked.

"Patience, Doctor Jones," said Wong. "Penny saved is penny earned."

"Another proverb?"

He nodded. "Very wise of you to notice. You are man we need."

"Need for what, Brother Wong?" I asked.

"Need go-between. Rupert Cornwall trust you. You will meet with him, learn about operation, report back to me. Then, when time is right, we strike."

"How long you figure this'll take?"

He shrugged. "Maybe week, maybe month, who know? Too many chefs spoil the soup."

"I don't know, Brother Wong," I said. "After all, I only got twenty-five days left to serve."

He broke out into a great big grin. "You not acquainted with Chinese calendar, I take it?"

"How long is twenty-five days on a Chinese calendar?" I asked.

He shrugged again. "Maybe week, maybe month, who know?" He looked across the desk at me. "We have deal?"

I sighed. "We have a deal."

"Good. Knew I could count on man of cloth."

"How do I report to you?" I asked.

"He know what I look like, so you will report to me through sons."

"I don't know how to break this unhappy tiding to you, Brother Wong," I said, "but I ain't got no sons."

"I have twenty-eight," he replied distastefully. "All currently unemployed and available to work for honorable father."

"Twenty-eight?" I repeated. "I don't envy your missus none."

"Have seventeen missuses," he answered. "Fifteen currently suing for back alimony. That's why move here from Honolulu."

"My heart bleeds for you, Brother Wong," I said with as much sincerity as I could muster on the spur of the moment.

"Whenever I become depressed over situation, I just remember old Chinese proverb: Watched pot never boil." He got to his feet and walked around the desk to stand in front of me. "I think for this case we use Number Nine and Number Twenty-six sons."

"What are their names?"

"Just told you: Nine and Twenty-six. Ran out of names after Number Five son was born."

"What do you call your daughters—A through Z?"

Wong threw back his head and laughed. "You fine fellow, Doctor Jones. Wonderful sense of humor. Sincerely hope Rupert Cornwall not cut your tongue out before case is over."

"Uh . . . let's just pause a second for serious reflection, Brother Wong," I said. "Old Rupert wouldn't really cut my tongue out, would he?"

"No, not really," said Wong.

"That's better."

"Would have one of his hired killers do it for him."

"You know," I said, "upon further consideration, I think the Lord would want me to serve out my full sentence. After all, I was caught fair and square, and somehow this seems unfair to the just and honorable man who sentenced me."

"Whatever you say, Doctor Jones," said Wong. He went back around the desk, opened the drawer, and pulled out a sheet of paper that was subdivided into hundreds of little squares. "This help you pass the time."

"What is it?" I asked.

He smiled. "Calendar of Chinese week." He tossed me a pencil. "You can mark off each day with this. Will bring new one when you run out of lead."

Which is how I became an operative in the employ of the Hong Kong police.

You'd think that the biggest gangster in Hong Kong would operate out of one of them beautiful old palaces that overlook the ocean, or failing that he'd set up headquarters in a penthouse suite in some luxury hotel. So you can imagine my surprise when I wandered down a couple of back alleyways and found Rupert Cornwall's place of business to be a run-down little storefront right between a fish peddler and a shirtmaker.

The whole area smelled of incense and dead fish, and there were lots of tall men dressed in black and wearing lean and hungry looks, but I just ignored 'em all like the God-fearing Christian gentleman that I am and walked up to Cornwall's door and pounded on it a couple of times. A muscular guy who looked like a cross between an Olympic weightlifter and a small mountain, let me in and ushered me through a maze of unopened cardboard boxes to a back room, where Rupert Cornwall sat in an easy chair, smoking a Havana cigar and going through the Hong Kong version of the *Daily Racing Form*.

"Doctor Jones!" he said. "My dear fellow, I hadn't expected to see you again for almost a month!" He paused and looked around. "We just moved in here a few days ago. I used to operate out of one of the hotels, but my overhead was killing me."

"Yeah, I know how expensive them luxury suites can be," I agreed.

"Luxury suites nothing," he corrected me. "It was making bail two and three times a day. Ah, well, you're here, and that's all that matters." Suddenly his eyes narrowed. "Just how, exactly, did you get here so soon?"

"I'm a fast walker, Brother Rupert," I answered.

"I thought you were incarcerated for thirty days."

I shrugged. "Time flies when you're having fun. I guess I'd been there longer than I thought."

"Yes, I saw little Mei Sung," he said with a grin. "Well, are you prepared to discuss the details of our first business venture?"

"That's what I'm here for, Brother Rupert," I said.

"Fine," he said. "I want you to know up front that I am an honest businessman who would never dream of harming another soul, Doctor Jones."

"I could tell that right off," I said.

"I seek no commendation for my work," he continued. "I'm in the import/export business, hardly a noteworthy or romantic occupation. I pay my bills on time, I treat my help well, I have virtually no social life, I avoid the spotlight at all costs. In point of fact, I am a laissez-faire capitalist of the highest order. And yet, there is a local official who has harassed me, threatened me, tried to drive me out of business, and caused me a considerable loss of revenue."

"No!" I said, shocked.

"Yes, Doctor Jones," he replied. "I have borne his enmity silently up to now, but he has become an intolerable nuisance, and it is my intention to so embarrass him that he is forced to resign from his position, if not leave Hong Kong altogether."

"What does this have to do with *me*, Brother Rupert?" I asked.

"I cannot proceed with my plan alone. For your complicity in ridding me of this vile and obdurate man, I am willing to pay you the sum of one thousand British pounds sterling. What do you say to that?"

"That's a right tidy sum," I allowed. "Just who is this here villain that we plan to put out of commission?"

"A man named Wong."

"Would that be Inspector Willie Wong of the Hong Kong Police?" I suggested.

"The very same. How is it that you come to know his name, Doctor Jones?"

"Oh, they bandy it around a lot down at the jail," I said.

"Have you any compunctions in helping me rid decent society of this man?"

"Not a one," I said. "Why, did you know that every single man he arrested swore that he was innocent? We certainly can't have a man like that riding roughshod over the people of this fair city."

He broke out into a great big smile. "I believe we understand each other perfectly, Doctor Jones. I *knew* I had selected the right man!"

"How do we plan to deal with this menace to social stability and free enterprise?" I asked.

"Willie Wong's reputation rests on the fact that he has never made a mistake, never arrested an innocent man, never let a guilty one get away," said Cornwall, puffing on his cigar. "If we can publicly embarrass and humiliate him, I believe his honor will demand that he retire from public service."

"And just how do we aim to do that?"

"I have it on good authority that the Empire Emerald, the largest gemstone in all of China, will be stolen from the Fung Ping Shan Museum tomorrow night," he said, leaning forward in his chair. "I will arrange that every clue points toward you, and knowing Wong, he will almost certainly bring you into custody within hours of the robbery. It will then be revealed that he has wrongly arrested a man of God, and that, furthermore, the emerald was stolen by one of his own sons." He leaned back with a satisfied smile. "What do you think of that?"

"I think I want five hundred pounds up front and the name of a good bondsman, just in case something goes wrong," I said.

"Certainly, my dear Doctor Jones." He pulled out a wallet thick enough to choke a small elephant and peeled off five one-hundred-pound notes, which he then handed over to me. "I distrust a man who doesn't look out for his own interest."

"Okay," I said, stuffing the money into my pocket. "What else do I have to know or do?"

"Very little," he said. "Spend an hour browsing at the museum late tomorrow afternoon, perhaps get into a slight altercation with one of the tourists so people will remember seeing you there, keep off the streets between midnight and two o'clock in the morning, and put *this* in a safe place."

With that, he handed me a small cloth bag that was closed with a drawstring.

"What's in it?" I asked.

"Take a look."

I opened it up, and found a lump of coal about the size of a golf ball.

"*That*, Doctor Jones, will prove to be the undoing of Willie Wong. Hide it well, but not so well that a thorough search cannot turn it up. While you are spending the night in jail and his men are ransacking your room, my own operatives will plant the real emerald on one of his brats."

"An emerald this big is an awful high price to pay to get rid of one bothersome policeman," I said.

"He costs me more than that every week," said Cornwall. "It will be money well spent."

"Well, considering that it ain't yours to begin with, I reckon I can see the logic in that," I agreed.

"And now, Doctor Jones, it is best that we part company. I don't want anyone to know that we've been in contact since my release from jail." He stood up and walked me to the door. "Your remaining five hundred pounds will be delivered in an envelope to your hotel the morning after your arrest, and you will be contacted later in the week concerning our next venture."

"Sounds good to me, Brother Rupert," I said, shaking his hand. "It's always nice to do business with a Christian gentleman like yourself."

"We've lots more business to do when this sordid little affair is over," he said with a twinkle in his eye.

I kind of doubted it, since he never asked me what hotel he was supposed to deliver my money to. But with five hundred pounds in my pocket and Willie Wong on my side, I decided that things were definitely looking up for the Tabernacle of Saint Luke.

* * *

I had walked maybe half a mile from Cornwall's office when I saw two young Chinamen staring at me from a street corner, so I strolled over to them.

"Nine?" I said to the bigger one.

There was no response.

"Twenty-six?" I said.

"Make it thirty and you've got yourself a date," he said with a giggle.

"Doctor Jones!" yelled a young man from across the street. "We're over here!"

I turned and saw two more Chinamen and made a beeline toward them.

"Are you Willie Wong's kids?" I asked.

The older one nodded. "We've got orders to take you to Dad."

"Lead the way," I said.

I followed them a couple of blocks to a dimly lit restaurant. They left me at the door, and as I entered it I saw Wong nod to me from a table in the back.

"You visit with Mr. Rupert Cornwall, yes?" he said, gesturing me to sit down.

"Yeah. He doesn't like you much."

"Stitch in time save nine."

"You ever consider writing a Chinese proverb book?" I asked him.

"Please continue," he said, slurping his soup.

"Near as I can make out, he plans to steal the Empire Emerald around midnight tomorrow."

"Ah, so."

"Not only that," I added. "But he plans to make it look like *I* stole it, and while you're busy arresting me he's going to plant it on one of your sons."

"Very interesting," he said with no show of interest whatsoever.

"Well, that's it. I'm done now, right?" I said. "I mean, you'll be waiting for him at the museum, and I can go off converting all you godless yellow heathen—no offense intended—and maybe build my tabernacle."

"Not that easy," said Wong.

"Why not?" I demanded.

"Cannot make omelet without breaking eggs."

"What the hell is that supposed to mean?"

"So sorry," he said. "Wrong proverb." He paused and tried again. "Beauty only skin deep."

"Well, that explains everything," I said.

"Cannot capture Mr. Rupert Cornwall at museum where emerald reside," continued Wong as he finished his soup.

"I already told you what time he's going to show up."

"*He* will not steal emerald. He will have underling do so. I do not want little fish while big fish lead horse to water but cannot make him drink."

"So what *do* you plan to do?"

"Mr. Rupert Cornwall expect me to arrest you. I will not disappoint him."

"That may not disappoint *him*," I said, "but it'll disappoint the hell out of *me*."

He shook his head. "Just go through motions. Then catch him when he try to plant emerald on honorable son."

"What if he has a henchman do *that*, too?" I asked.

"Almost certainly will. After all, home is where heart is."

"I don't think you understand me, Brother Wong," I said. "What's the difference if you catch a henchman stealing the emerald or you catch one planting it on your kid?"

"Much easier to trace emerald back to Mr. Rupert Cornwall *after* he has stolen it than before," explained Wong.

"And what happens to me?" I asked.

"We arrest you with much fanfare in afternoon, release you when we apprehend henchman that night."

Then a particularly bothersome thought occurred to me.

"What if he changes his mind and decides to keep the emerald?"

"Then you have lied to me, I take full credit for capturing you, city give another medal to humble detective, and I apprehend Mr. Rupert Cornwall some other day." He smiled. "You see, either way it all work out."

Well, I could see it all working out for Willie Wong and Rupert Cornwall a lot easier than it all working out for me, so me and the Lord decided that it was time to take matters into our own hands, and what we did was this: I went out shopping at a bunch of costume jewelry stores, and when I finally came to a fake emerald about the size of the lump of coal I was toting around in the little cloth bag, I bought it for twenty pounds and tucked it away in my pocket.

Then I went over to Bonham Road and visited the Fung Ping Shan Museum a day early, found the Empire Emerald, and tried to figure out how to substitute my stone for the real one, but since I'm a God-fearing Christian missionary who ain't never had an illegal impulse in my life, I finally had to admit that while the trip wires and the lock on the front door wouldn't give me no problems, the alarm built into the case was a type I hadn't seen before and there was just no way I was going to be able to switch the emeralds without setting it off and waking up such dead as weren't otherwise occupied at the time.

One thing I did notice, though, was that the guards were Brits and not Chinamen, so I waited until they locked up the museum and followed one of them home. I got his name off the mailbox, and early the next morning, right after he'd left for work, I called his wife and told her that my shop had inadvertently ruined her husband's tuxedo, but that we would be happy to make amends. She explained that he didn't *have* a tuxedo, and I told her I was sure it was his but just to make doubly certain I needed to know the name of the establishment she did her business with, and as soon as she told me I popped over there and informed them I was a visiting relative who had been sent by to pick up any uniforms he might have left there. Sure enough, they had one, all bright and green and neatly pressed, with shining brass buttons. I tipped them a couple of pounds, took it to the men's room in the back of a nearby tavern, and slipped it on—and an hour later I was patrolling the corridors of the museum, nodding pleasantly to passersby and keeping a watchful eye on the emerald.

Then, when the museum hit a slow period and the room containing the Empire Emerald had emptied out, I walked into it with a beer in my hand, set it down atop the glass case that covered the gemstone, and tipped the bottle over. I pulled the phony emerald out of my pocket, lifted up the glass cover, and as the alarm went off I quickly exchanged it for the real emerald, got down on my knees, pulled out a handkerchief, and set about trying to clean the beer off the glass.

The room filled up to overflowing with guards about ten seconds later. A couple of them even covered me with their pistols until they saw the emerald where it ought to be, and then they helped me put the glass cover back on. I explained that I was new on the job, and that I was just trying to clean up after myself because I had spilled some beer, and after telling me what a clumsy fool I was, they told me to pack up my gear and go home, that my services were no longer needed. They managed to get the alarm turned off just about the time I was coming down the museum steps to the sidewalk in front of the building.

I went back to my room at the Luk Kwok Hotel, where I had a little chat with my Silent Partner, explaining to Him that while what I did may have seemed a criminal act on the surface of it, if He would examine the consequences carefully He would have to agree that it was for the best all the way around. Willie Wong was still going to capture Rupert Cornwall, so *he* would be happy; the museum would never know they weren't displaying the real Empire Emerald, so *they* would be happy; Cornwall was going to go to jail anyway, so at least he wouldn't be any *less* happy for not having the emerald in his possession for a couple of minutes. And me, I finally had sufficient capital to build the Tabernacle of Saint Luke, which I promised the Lord I would do just as soon as I spent a few years scouting out the territory for the very best location.

Everything went pretty smoothly the next day. First thing I did was stop by the laundry and drop off the uniform, so no one would notice it was missing and maybe start thinking about *why* it was missing. Then I scouted up some lunch that didn't smell of fish, and wandered the streets a bit, and at about two in the afternoon I walked over to the museum, lingered there for an hour or two, had a very public misunderstanding with a blonde Frenchwoman, and then headed back toward the Luk Kwok.

Along the way, I picked up some chewing gum and stuck a wad of it into my mouth. Then I stopped by a little gift shop, and while the proprietor was speaking to another customer, I stuck the Empire Emerald on the back of his radiator with the chewing gum. Since it was midsummer, I knew he wasn't going to fiddle with the radiator for another few months, and I figured to be back for it within just a day or two. The very last thing I did was hide the cloth bag with the lump of coal inside the water tank behind the toilet once I returned to my room in the Luk Kwok. Then I lay back on my bed, pulled out the Good Book, and whiled the night away reading about Solomon's more exotic dalliances.

The police showed up right on schedule, at a quarter after two in the morning, and hustled me off to jail. I kept protesting my innocence, the way I figured both Willie Wong and Rupert Cornwall would expect of me, and then, just after daybreak, a guard came and unlocked my cell. As far as I was concerned he could have waited another couple of hours, since I hadn't yet got around to converting Mei Sung again, but given the circumstances I didn't think it proper to protest, so I let him escort me to freedom, which turned out to be Wong's little cubbyhole.

"Good morning, Doctor Jones," he said without getting up from his chair.

"Good morning, Brother Wong," I said. "How'd it go last night?"

"Apprehend whole gang," he said happily. "Rupert Cornwall in cell one flight up from yours."

"That's great news, Brother Wong," I said. "And did you get the emerald back?"

"Empire Emerald once again on display in Fung Ping Shan Museum."

"I guess that closes the case."

He nodded. "Cannot teach old dog new tricks."

"Well, I'll sure remember that the next time I run into an old dog, Brother Wong," I said. "I assume I'm free to go."

"Farther you go, the better."

"I beg your pardon?"

"It best you leave Hong Kong," said Wong. "Many friends and clients of Rupert Cornwall not very pleased with you."

"A telling point," I agreed. "Gimme just a couple of hours to get my gear together and I'll be off."

"Thank you for help, Doctor Jones," said Wong. "Knew you were right man for job."

"My pleasure, Brother Wong," I said.

Then I took my leave of him, went back to the Luk Kwok, and looked around to see if there was anything I wanted to take along with me. There were some old shirts and pants and socks and such, but since I was about to pick up the Empire Emerald on my way out of town, I decided that I really owed myself a new wardrobe, so I finally left empty-handed.

I moseyed over to the area where the gift shop was, did maybe an hour of serious window-shopping up and down the street for the benefit of anyone who might have been watching me, and finally entered the little store after I was sure I wasn't being observed.

"You are Lucifer Jones, are you not?" asked the proprietor the second I closed the door behind me.

"How did you know?" I asked. "I don't recall talking to you last night."

"I was given your description by Inspector Wong," he replied. "He left a note for you."

He handed me a folded-up piece of paper, which I opened and read:

Dear Doctor Jones:

Had feeling all along you were perfect man for job. Had honorable Number Ten, Fourteen, Seventeen, and Twenty-Two sons observe you constantly since you left custody. Not only is Rupert Cornwall under arrest, but we now know weakness in museum security system, all thanks to you.

*Is old Chinese custom to exchange gifts.
You will know where to look for yours.*

> *Your humble servant,
> Willie Wong,
> Hong Kong Police*

P.S. Money is root of all evil.

I threw the paper down on the counter and raced over to the radiator. I reached behind it, found my gum and the stone, and pulled it out: it was the same lump of coal Rupert Cornwall had given me two days ago.

"Is something wrong, Mr. Jones?" asked the storekeeper.

"Nothing I shouldn't have expected from trusting someone who ain't a decent, God-fearing Christian," I said bitterly. "Give me a map, brother."

"A map?" he repeated.

"This town's seen the last of me," I said. "I'm heading to where a man of the cloth can convert souls in peace and quiet without worrying about getting flimflammed by gangsters and detectives and the like."

He pulled a map out from behind the counter. I looked at it for a minute and then, with four hundred and fifty pounds of Rupert Cornwall's money still in my pocket, I lit out across the mouth of the Pearl River for Macao, where I hoped to find a better class of sinner to listen to my preaching.